Ruins

Julia Edwards was born in 1977. She lives in Salisbury with her husband and three sons, and feels increasingly outnumbered.

The Ring from the Ruins is the seventh and final book in *The Scar Gatherer* series, a sequence of adventure novels about time-travel.

To find out more, please visit: *www.scaragatherer.co.uk*.

C016791734

Also by Julia Edwards

Other titles in The Scar Gatherer series
The Leopard in the Golden Cage
Saving the Unicorn's Horn
The Falconer's Quarry
The Demon in the Embers
Slaves for the Isabella
The Shimmer on the Glass

For adults

Time was Away

The Ring from the Ruins

Julia Edwards

Published in the United Kingdom by:

Laverstock Publishing
129 Church Road, Laverstock, Salisbury,
Wiltshire, SP1 1RB, UK

First printed October 2019

Cover design by Peter O'Connor
www.bespokebookcovers.com

ISBN: 978-0-9928443-9-4

For more information about the series, please visit
www.scargatherer.co.uk

For Rick Boden and his Pierre Tempête,
who changed my life more than
either of us realised!

ACKNOWLEDGEMENTS

This is the end of a long road. My husband is still feeding me and my parents are still cheering me on, but now I have a huge crowd of children behind me too, asking me when the next book is coming and what it will be about. It's a much better place to be!

My particular thanks for this book go to Phil Greenough, an Everton supporter who managed to get past the opening of the book to provide some very useful observations about wartime Liverpool; Ernie Jackson, who grew up in Bootle just a few streets away from Lucy, and who generously shared with me all kinds of recollections from his childhood during the Liverpool Blitz; and Christine Huard, the former Ofsted Inspector who kindly volunteered to take a look at this book after helping me with both *Slaves for the Isabella* and *The Shimmer on the Glass.* This is a much better book as a result of their help.

I would also like to thank the children and staff of Bemerton St. John Primary School and Broad Chalke Primary School for being so enthusiastic every time I gave them updates on the book's progress, and for their feedback on the draft version. Any remaining errors are my own.

1

"Is your mobile safe, Joe?" Uncle Nick asked, as Anfield football stadium loomed ahead of them. "Match day crowds attract pickpockets, you know."

Joe nodded and tightened his grip on his cross-body bag.

"Why did you bring that?" Dad frowned. "Couldn't you have just carried your water bottle?"

"This is my Liverpool bag," Joe said stubbornly. "Nick gave it to me for my birthday."

"That's right, it's my fault." Nick grinned. "I bought it at the last match I came to. I was going to get you a rucksack, but that would have been too big to take in."

"You don't have anything valuable in it, do you?" Dad persisted.

"No," Joe said. "Just the bottle and my mobile."

"You'd be better off with that inside your coat if you've got a pocket in there," Nick said. "Where's yours, Sam?"

Joe's brother pulled his phone out of the back of his jeans with a sheepish smile.

"Honestly!" Nick laughed. "How clueless are you?"

While they walked on, Joe unzipped his bag. Taking out his phone, he found the chain of his St. Christopher caught around it. Perhaps he shouldn't have brought it with him this afternoon, but he hadn't dared leave it at Nick's house in case he forgot it when they went home tomorrow. Besides, what was the point of having it if it always stayed on the bedside table?

All the same, he was glad he'd noticed. The necklace might easily have fallen out otherwise. It would be a disaster to lose it here in Liverpool, and even if he didn't lose it, dropping it could be nearly as bad. If it took him back into the past right now, while he was up on his feet, he'd be almost sure to collapse as he came back afterwards. That would mean another afternoon wasted in A&E for no reason like he'd had in London once with Mum. He and Dad would miss the game. Joe didn't want that.

He dropped the St. Christopher back into the bag. It had lived at the bottom of one bag or another ever since Cornwall, so he always had it with him. There was no knowing when the next chance would come to get into one of Lucy's worlds, but he hadn't dared wear the necklace since the ordeal of the shipwreck in the summer. Keeping it in the bag was a

10

way of keeping it under control.

He hurried to catch up with the others, wondering if the St. Christopher counted as something valuable, since Dad had asked. To Joe, it was unimaginably precious, but that was because of its magic. It was unlikely to be worth much to someone pinching it to sell on, even though it was made of silver, since the magic wouldn't work for anyone else.

Or would it? For the first time ever, it dawned on Joe that the St. Christopher might have the power to take anybody who had it back into the past. He'd always assumed it was only him, but there was no reason why it wouldn't work for everyone. If somebody stole it, then dropped it, they might easily end up in the past like he had done. Maybe they would even find themselves with Lucy!

Joe felt a sharp pang. He hadn't seen Lucy for over three months, not since the middle of August. Of course, during the last two years there had been longer periods than that when he hadn't seen her. This time, though, he'd missed her more than ever before. He'd spent hours online hunting unsuccessfully for the photograph of her that had been taken in Porthkellow. It probably didn't exist any more, but he couldn't bring himself to admit defeat yet.

Inside the stadium, the excitement was building. Joe picked his way along the row of seats behind Nick and Sam. His uncle was a fanatical Liverpool supporter and had been promising them for years that he'd take them to Anfield one day to watch a match. Hearing a chant start up at the other end of the pitch, Joe's chest tightened in excitement. That day had finally come!

He sat down, thinking how different it was being here rather than on the sofa at Dad's. The roar of all those voices together was familiar, but the atmosphere buzzed in a way you couldn't feel through the TV. As the match kicked off, the air seemed to thicken with the willpower of thousands of people urging their team to score quickly and take the lead.

After a while though, the tension started to ebb away. There were no goals on either side, nor even any near misses. Nick muttered and groaned, and shouted when one of his favourite players got injured. Sam and Dad were riveted, but Joe's attention began to drift. He flicked through the match programme, looking at the photos and information about the Liverpool players. They were an international bunch, very few British players and almost as many black players as white. What would the footmen from Lucy's household in Bristol make of this, he wondered wryly. It showed how much the world had changed in the last two hundred years.

At half-time, Nick suggested they stay put. There wasn't long enough to get anything to eat or drink, he said. They'd just spend the whole time queuing. Joe delved in his bag for a pen so he could write in his programme. While he was looking for the right page, two men from further along the row squeezed past. The second man's coat brushed against Joe's bag. It tipped over.

The water bottle thudded as it hit the floor. To Joe's horror, there was a tinkling sound like a coin bouncing, far away below him. His head filled with the familiar hissing noise. He bent hastily, as though to pick up his St. Christopher. It wouldn't be there. He knew that already.

The ground wasn't there either. Joe's hand reached out into empty space in front of him. His feet were hanging in mid-air. His stomach lurched. He straightened up slowly, carefully.

It was dark without the glare of the stadium lights, and very quiet. There was a smell of coal smoke on the air that told him he was in the past again, another of Lucy's worlds presumably. But when?

He felt around, trying to work out what he was sitting on. It wasn't a seat. It felt rough, like a wooden plank. He shivered. It was colder than it had been a few moments ago, or perhaps he just wasn't as warmly dressed. He realised he could feel the surface of the wood behind his knees but not at his calves. He patted his legs with his hands. He was wearing shorts and long socks, a combination he'd only ever worn for football. These were too stiff to be football shorts though, and the shoes on his feet were lace-up leather boots.

He moved his hands methodically up his body, trying to keep his alarm in check. As usual, the time slip had happened at a moment when he wasn't expecting it, so he hadn't been ready. Somehow, he never was! He gritted his teeth and concentrated on his clothes: a thin coat over a sleeveless knitted jumper; and a shirt with the knot of a tie at the collar, like he wore for school.

He frowned, trying to think when boys had worn this sort of thing. It might be the 1950s, or perhaps earlier. What about the Second World War? Had he landed in Liverpool during World War Two? That might be more exciting than he'd bargained for! Still, he'd survived the Great Fire of London. Why shouldn't he survive a few bombs?

Peering around, he noticed that it wasn't as dark as he'd originally thought. There was a roof directly above him, but now that his eyes had adjusted, he could see sky ahead. Was this still the football stadium though? Every other time he'd arrived in the past, he'd started out in exactly the same place as he'd been in his own world, at the same time of day, the same day of the year. It might well be around four o'clock on the twenty-sixth of November, but he couldn't see the football pitch. Instead, there were huge stacks of bricks, heaps of corrugated iron, and towering piles of wood around him, as though Anfield had become a giant builders' yard.

Cautiously, he set about climbing down from the

timber stack he was perched on. He expected someone to yell at him that he shouldn't be here, but nobody did. As he clambered down, he listened intently in case he dislodged something. A few planks would be enough to kill him if they fell from the top of a pile this high. By the time he reached the ground, his hands were cold and sore and his legs were trembling.

It was gloomy down here. Joe rubbed his eyes and blinked. His St. Christopher must be somewhere nearby, though he realised it had fallen from quite a height. That was why the tinkling had sounded distant. He tried to think whether he'd heard the pendant roll after it stopped bouncing, but of course, the rushing in his ears had drowned out all other noise.

He got down on his hands and knees. He couldn't see the necklace anywhere. If the disk had come off the chain, it might easily have rolled underneath one of the stacks. He gulped. Even though it had already worked its magic to bring him here, he couldn't afford to lose it.

He took a deep breath and let it out slowly. Maybe he was carrying a torch. He tried the pockets of his shorts but found only a bit of string and a cotton handkerchief. He dug his hands into his coat pockets. This time, he brought out a battered box of matches and a stub of candle. He couldn't imagine carrying these sorts of things around with him at home, but right now they were exactly what he needed.

He glanced about to make sure there wasn't

anything he might set fire to by mistake, then struck a match. It went out. He struck a second, cupping his hand to shield the tiny flame, and was about to use it to light the candle when a glint caught his eye. He sprang towards it. The match went out, but his fingers were already closing around the St. Christopher. What luck! Just a few centimetres to the right and it would have disappeared under railway sleepers!

He hung it around his neck and fastened the catch of the new chain. Tobias had broken the last one on the beach in Porthkellow, which had already been the fourth replacement. Joe grinned. After the second one had got broken in Jorvik, he'd bought another five. He couldn't have said why at the time, but it felt now as though he'd known he would need them! He stuffed the St. Christopher down behind his collar, glad to feel the cold silver against his skin again.

Now he could turn his attention to getting out of here. Assuming this was still Anfield, Nick had led them to their seats from the right. Joe looked that way, but couldn't see anything except building materials. He remembered following Nick for some distance beneath the stands. That meant the entrance wasn't necessarily to the right at all. He would just have to make his way around the stadium until he found it.

He scrambled past bricks and between heaps of metal girders, feeling his way more than seeing it. The construction jungle seemed to go on and on. Perhaps he was going the wrong way.

He changed direction. It was no better. In fact, he was in danger of going round and round in circles. He stopped and looked carefully at where the light was coming from, then set off once more.

A minute or two later, he came to the back of what looked like football terraces. This stand was much smaller than any of them were in his own time, only deep enough for a dozen rows at most, and there were no seats. Through it, however, he spied the open grass, empty and grey-green in the twilight. He swung himself up on the railings, grateful to have found something that made sense, then climbed over and trotted down to the edge of the pitch.

Out in the open, it was noticeable how much darker the sky was than it had been a few minutes ago. Joe's anxiety reared up again. He had to get out quickly if he didn't want to spend the night here with nothing to eat and no blankets. Even once he'd escaped, he wouldn't have long to find Lucy before night fell. He had no idea where to look for her either, no strategy except trusting to luck.

He gave himself a shake. It was no good thinking like that. He scanned the stadium, trying to guess which corner of the pitch was most likely to be the exit. Unable to decide, he set off towards the nearest one, and to his relief, soon spotted a pair of tall gates through the gloom between the stands. He quickened his pace. As he drew near, however, he saw that they were fastened with a heavy chain and padlock.

He halted, dismayed. Of course the football ground was locked up! Whoever owned all the stuff stored here wouldn't want it to disappear!

He prowled around the entrance area, looking for another way out. There was a small gap at the top of the gates, but it was going to be hard work shimmying up them, and harder still squeezing through. Other ways out would almost certainly be just as difficult, though. He braced himself, then went at the gates with determination.

A few minutes later, he was standing breathless but triumphant on the other side. His fingers were numb, his shins bruised, and he'd ripped the pocket of his coat. It was just as well Mum wasn't around to tell him off.

The next moment, he wished she was. A man was advancing on him. He was wearing a khaki uniform and a tin hat with the letter 'W' painted on it.

"What do you think you're doing, boy?" he snapped. "I saw you, sneaking out of there!"

"I – er…" Joe stammered. "I was just trying to get back something I'd dropped. A while ago," he added.

"Something you'd dropped?" the man repeated. "A likely story!" He was carrying a flashlight that he swung now in the direction of the gates. He flicked it on for a few seconds, and then off again. "Where's the rest of your gang?" He glared at Joe.

Automatically, Joe turned to look over his shoulder. "Gang?" he echoed.

"The other mischief-makers! You're not the first I've seen coming out of there."

"There wasn't anyone else in there just now," Joe said, confused. He wondered if he knew this man. He had a strong sense of having been told off by him before.

"Not now, stupid boy! On other occasions. It's a disgrace, young hooligans running wild everywhere! You should have stayed away in the country, where you were evacuated. It was madness to allow you home with no schools to go to." He snorted. "It's time the authorities clamped down. I've a good mind to haul you along to the police station!"

"I wasn't doing any harm!" Joe cried. "I didn't damage anything. There's nobody with me." He heard the note of misery in his own voice at this last statement.

"You were stealing, then!"

Joe spread his arms wide. "What could I have stolen from in there?"

"Turn out your pockets!" barked the man.

Joe did so, glad that he already knew what was in them.

The man surveyed the things in Joe's hands. "Where's your identity card?"

Joe looked down. He was sure there hadn't been one. "Er ... at home," he lied.

"What good is it at home? You must carry it with you at all times!" The man's eyebrows drew together into a single, bristly grey caterpillar. "And what was it you were supposedly looking for? None of this, I'll be bound!"

Joe swiftly considered showing him the St. Christopher, and just as swiftly decided against it. "I couldn't find it," he said, feigning disappointment. "It was a lucky charm."

"Well, think yourself lucky that I'm prepared to let you go," the man growled. "Don't let me catch you sneaking in or out of there again. I come this way every day, and I never forget a face!" He turned on his heel and marched off.

Joe stood watching him go. He felt slightly stunned. Nick had always reckoned Liverpudlians had a great sense of humour. Well, not now they didn't!

Maybe it was just that particular man. The familiarity nagged at Joe. Perhaps he was someone from long, long ago. Joe just hoped he wouldn't meet him again, whoever he was.

He looked up and down the street, trying to work out which way to go. In front of the stadium in his own world there had been an open plaza and a building site, and beyond that, wasteland ready for further development. Now, however, he was standing on a pavement with some small houses to his right, and a row of old-fashioned shops on the other side of the road. At either end of the shops, long terraces of houses stretched away down side-streets in the dusk.

It was almost dark now. He'd assumed it would be brighter out here than it had been inside the football ground. There was a lamp post right beside him with a white line painted round it, but the light wasn't lit. Nor were any of the other street lamps. The shops were in darkness too, and there were no cars on the road. In his own world, there would have been a constant hum of traffic from further away, even if the street was quiet for a moment. Here, the only vehicle was an ancient van parked beside the kerb. The place felt deserted. Even the few people who passed him kept their heads down as though hurrying away from something.

Joe stepped off the pavement to cross the road. He had no idea where he was going, but there was no point standing around.

Out of the corner of his eye, he saw a pool of light speeding along the ground towards him. Then there was a cry and a high-pitched squeal.

Something hit him hard.

2

Joe lay sprawled on the road, the breath knocked out of him.

For a few moments, he couldn't think what had just happened. His ribcage felt as though it had been bounced against a wall. His palms smarted and his cheek stung. He listened anxiously for the rushing of air in his ears, in case he was about to be thrown back into his own world. That would be infuriating, when he hadn't yet found Lucy! All was quiet, however.

A groan came from nearby. He raised his head to see a girl uncrumpling herself from the road. A bike lay twisted on the ground next to her, its wheel jammed in a pothole.

Joe got to his feet. Something trickled from his knee towards his sock. He dug out his handkerchief and dabbed at the blood. "I'm really sorry," he said to the girl. "I didn't see you in time. Your light is pointing at the ground."

The girl dusted herself down. "Of course it is!"

she said crossly, stooping to pick up her satchel. "Where've you been the last year?" She examined the wheel of the bike. "Oh no! The tyre's burst!"

"I really am sorry," Joe said again. He peered at her face. Hope had leapt in him at the sound of her voice, though the Liverpool accent was new. Could this really be Lucy? He could hardly believe his luck, finding her already in a city this big!

"The tyre's not your fault," the girl said. She tucked her dark hair behind her ears. It had been cut short, in a bob. It suited her, Joe thought, which was more than could be said for the brown coat and skirt she had on. She sounded dismayed now rather than cross. For his own part, Joe had to make an effort to contain his excitement. This was definitely her! Lucy! His best friend!

"The roads are awful, aren't they?" she was saying. "I know the authorities have more than enough to do, what with Jerry making new craters every few nights. But I still wish they'd fix the potholes!"

Joe put his blood-smeared handkerchief back in his pocket. Who was Jerry, he wondered. Was Lucy talking about the Germans? That had been the British nickname for them in both world wars. 'Jerry making craters' might be the Germans dropping bombs. The man who'd just told him off had been in some sort of military uniform, too, so his guess had probably been right: this was the Second World War. He felt a flash of satisfaction.

"It's going to take me ages to get home now!" Lucy said. "I'll be in real trouble if there isn't time to mend the tyre. My brother's on duty tonight, and this is his bike. I only borrowed it to get to my lessons this afternoon."

"On duty? Peter?" Joe frowned. Surely Lucy's brother was too young to have any official kind of job! Lucy herself looked the age Joe expected – she would be thirteen in March, the same as him – but that meant that her brother wasn't yet fifteen.

Lucy was staring at him. In spite of the gloom, Joe could see she'd gone pale. "How do you know he's called Peter?" she asked.

He gulped. If he'd needed confirmation that this was Lucy, then here it was. But that had been an idiotic slip! "I thought that was what you said," he fibbed, "when you looked at his bike." She hadn't, he knew very well. He just hoped she wasn't so sure.

"What does he do, on the bike?" he asked, hoping to distract her.

She was still wary. "I'm sure I didn't mention his name," she said. "He's in the Civil Defence Corps." For a moment, she studied Joe, then asked abruptly, "Where did you come from? Have you been away?"

"What?"

"I can see from your face, you don't know what the CDC is. Peter does night duty three times a week, carrying messages." She paused. When Joe said nothing, she went on, "He takes messages from the fire

24

watchers or the ARP wardens to the control centre, so they can send help to the right place." She looked at Joe through narrowed eyes. "Quite a lot of boys his age do it. How come you didn't know?"

Joe clenched his jaw. He might have managed to cover his original mistake, sort of, but it clearly wouldn't be long before Lucy was on to him. It sounded as though she was already starting to think he was a half-wit. It was infuriating how this always happened, in every world!

Perhaps he should tell her the truth, right now. At least then he could explain his ignorance of her time. He could tell her one or two things about his own world too. After all, there was plenty she wouldn't have a clue about. It would be so pleasing to turn the tables on her!

It took less than a second for Joe to relinquish the idea. It was much too early to tell her who he really was, however much he might like to get it out of the way. In the meantime, he had to come up with a story she would believe.

"You're right, I've only just got here," he said, deciding to start from the small pieces of truth he could use. "I have an uncle in Liverpool."

Lucy cocked her head to one side. "But you're from the south, aren't you? You don't speak like us. Are you from London? Were you evacuated?"

Evacuated. The man in uniform had mentioned evacuation. That was the word for children being sent

25

to live in the countryside during the war, to keep them safe. He'd read about that in 'Goodnight, Mr Tom' last year, and there had been another book he'd read a few years ago, called 'Carrie's War'.

He nodded, and waited to see if Lucy would fill in some of his story with her guesses.

"Loads of us were as well," she said. "My whole school got sent to North Wales last September, two days before war broke out. Most of us were back by Christmas though, in plenty of time to enjoy the fireworks this autumn!" She glanced nervously at the sky. "I really should be going." She took hold of the handlebars and wrenched the wheel out of the pothole. "Which way were you heading?"

Joe hesitated. "I don't know," he said. He pleaded silently for her to invite him to go with her.

"You don't know? You mean you don't know where you are? Or you don't know where you're going? Don't you know where your uncle lives?" She sounded amused.

Joe decided to take the bull by the horns. "Could I come back with you, just for tonight? I haven't got his address, you see." He knew very well that one night might not be enough, but it would give him time to work out his story.

Lucy laughed out loud. "How did you think you were going to find him? Liverpool might not be as big as London, but it's no village!"

Suddenly, Joe had had enough of feeling stupid.

He couldn't change how unprepared he was when he turned up in the past, since he never knew when it would happen or what year it would be. But he could at least invent something to stop Lucy thinking he was a total jerk.

"I've never met them," he said tersely. "I wrote to my mother to ask where they lived. I don't know if she got the letter. If she answered, it might have been opened by the couple I was staying with. The man wouldn't have given it to me, once he'd got hold of it."

Lucy looked surprised. "Why not?"

' He was horrible," Joe improvised, "and his wife was nearly as bad. She was terrified of him, so she always did what he said. I stuck it for as long as I could, but in the end, I ran away." He looked sideways at Lucy and was relieved to find no sign of disbelief on her face.

"What did they do?" she asked.

"They made me sleep in the barn and wash in the animal trough." Joe felt himself warming to his theme. He was about to add that they'd starved him when he realised he probably looked too well fed for that. "Mr. Evans made me work from early in the morning until late at night," he said instead, using the name of the man in 'Carrie's War'. "He beat me most days, too. He was a slave-driver!"

He stopped short, wincing. He shouldn't have used a word like that, especially when it was a lie. After all, he'd met people in one of Lucy's other worlds who'd suffered at the hands of real slave-drivers. What would they think of him for talking like this?

"How did you keep your clothes so tidy?" Lucy asked. There was no mistrust in her tone, only curiosity.

Joe looked down at himself. "This was what I was wearing when I got there. They took these clothes away, and gave me others to wear that were hardly more than rags. The only time I wore these was when my mother came to visit."

"Why didn't you ask her to take you home with her? I would have!"

Joe put on a sorrowful expression. "I didn't want to let her down. She was so happy to think I was safe. I thought I might learn to bear it better." He shrugged. "It got worse, though. In the end, I stole my clothes back, and took some food and a little money from Mrs Evans' secret pot." He let his shoulders droop. "Poor Mrs Evans! I'd rather have taken her husband's money, but he kept it locked away."

"How did you get yourself here? Did you walk all the way? How far was it?" It was clear from Lucy's voice that she was impressed. For a moment, Joe wished it was all true. It would be good to impress her for real.

He shrugged again. "It's taken me just over a week," he said, hoping that sounded plausible. "In any case," he went on quickly, "until I find out where my uncle lives, I have nowhere to go."

Lucy nodded. "Of course you can come with

me. My name's Lucy, by the way. Lucy Lucas."

"Right. Pleased to meet you!" Joe smiled broadly.

"Pleased to meet you, too," she said, "though it would help if you told me your name!"

He blushed. "I'm Joe, short for Joseph," he said. "Joe Hopkins."

'Good. Hold the saddle for a minute, would you?" She went to the front of the bike and tried to straighten the wheel. It didn't budge. "Oh dear. It looks like we're going to have to walk and drag this thing along with us. I've never hit a pothole before. Trust a Londoner to push me into one!" She grinned at Joe.

Joe smiled back and felt a flutter inside him. Here he was again, with his dearest friend! It was wonderful to see her, even though she didn't remember him. He always regretted that, but he was used to it now. At least she seemed ready enough to like him this time.

The city was bizarrely quiet as they set off together through the back streets. People passed them now and then, men mostly, wearing flat caps and jackets, or sometimes longer coats and hats with brims. Occasionally, there were women in coats with trim waists. They wore brimmed hats too, making their faces difficult to see in the growing darkness. Some of them seemed to be carrying shopping in baskets or string bags.

There was still very little traffic. A few cars

went past with their lights angled down at the road, just like Lucy's lamp. Now and then, a bicycle whizzed by, and Joe could hear industrial clanking noises coming from some way away. Apart from that, however, there was no sound but the tap of their shoes on the pavement and the grinding of Lucy's crooked wheel.

Lucy was apparently cutting across the city on the most direct route home because she took them along one street of terraced houses after another. Joe began to wonder how she could be sure of where she was going. All the roads looked the same to him, and there were no street names at the junctions. Even when they crossed over bigger roads, there were no signs to indicate where they were or how to get to anywhere else.

Joe inspected the rows of houses they passed. The people who lived here were plainly far from rich, but they didn't seem to be as poor as Lucy's family had been in Cornwall either. The houses in each street were identical to each other, just one room wide with a dark bay window at the front and a tiny yard between the house and the pavement. There was no rubbish outside any of them, and with no cars parked on the road, it felt more spacious than streets like this in his own time. Almost every road had at least one squat brick building, similar to a block of garages, built right in the middle of the street. Joe was just wondering what they were when he saw something that stopped him in his tracks.

He stared. In the middle of one of the terraces

was a ragged gap where two houses should have been. All that was left was rubble and ruins: clusters of bricks and fallen timbers, a landslide of slates, floorboards that looked like they'd been thrown around, and part of what must have been a staircase.

Joe whistled through his teeth. These had been people's homes! As his gaze travelled up a fragment of wall, he realised he could make out the pattern of the wallpaper. High up on the wall was a strange purplish oval. It took Joe a moment to recognise it as a mirror reflecting the sky above next door's chimneys. How had it not shattered? And what had happened to the person who'd last looked in it?

"If the bomb's got your number, there's nothing you can do," Lucy said, answering Joe's unspoken question. "Just over a week ago, that was. The man was on fire duty at the docks. He left his wife and four children in the shelter he'd built under the stairs, came home the next morning to find his house gone and his whole family dead." She shook her head. "The neighbours were in one of these public air raid shelters." She gestured to the nearest squat building. "They survived, but they've lost everything."

She walked on again. Joe followed, but he couldn't resist looking back over his shoulder. He'd seen this sort of thing in black and white photos from the Blitz, but never in colour, never in real life!

"Didn't you see other bombsites as you walked through the city earlier?" Lucy asked. "There are streets around the docks that have been hit more than once."

"No," Joe said. Maybe it was unlikely, but he wasn't going to lie if he didn't have to.

They walked on for what seemed like a very long time. Part of the problem was that they couldn't walk quickly now that the last of the daylight had left the sky, because it was hard to see where they were going. Lucy's bicycle lamp cast a weak circle of light just in front of the wheel, but there was no other light.

Joe was struck by how strange it was to be in the middle of a city in such darkness. In any town in his own time, even in the smallest village, there would be lights everywhere, from cars, shops and pubs, street lamps, and the porches and windows of houses. Here, there was nothing, only white lines painted along the kerbs and around the unlit lamp posts and the trunks of trees on street corners, to stop you bumping into them. This was the black-out, he'd realised, keeping Britain dark to make it harder for enemy aeroplanes to find their targets. He'd read about it, but he'd never thought how difficult or depressing such darkness might be.

They didn't talk much as they walked. There was plenty Joe would have liked to ask about but didn't dare. Lucy had lapsed into silence after the first bombsite, and though they passed half a dozen more houses that had been bombed, she didn't stop.

At length, she said, "Nearly there, now." Then she froze. She put out a hand and caught Joe's sleeve.

"What? What's the matter?"

"Ssh." They were part way along yet another terraced street. She nodded towards one of the shelters in the middle of the road ahead of them. "Those men," she murmured.

Three shadowy figures were emerging from the building. The last closed the door quietly and carefully behind him.

"We'll carry on by as though we hadn't noticed," she whispered, "but stop next to the shelter."

Joe moved on beside Lucy. What was it about the men that had aroused her curiosity? Was it just that they'd come out of the air raid shelter? Surely it wasn't unreasonable for people to go inside even if there wasn't a raid happening?

As they drew level with the shelter, however, his heart missed a beat. All three had their collars turned up and their hats pulled down. In the stillness of the night, he could only just hear them muttering. Even so, he was almost certain he knew who they were. Two of them he'd last seen on a night nearly as dark as this, hooded and cloaked, about to trade in human lives. The third, he realised with a sinking heart, he'd encountered in every one of Lucy's worlds. Without a doubt, this was his great enemy, Tobias.

Joe's breath caught in his throat. Whatever these three were doing together, it would not be good.

3

Lucy drew the bike to a halt beside the building. Without the dragging of the damaged wheel, the night seemed unnaturally quiet. The muttering continued around the corner, however.

"Friday …" someone murmured. "… next drop."

Joe strained to hear.

"… you sure? What if –"

Abruptly, the men broke off. Joe turned his head and saw two figures approaching the way he and Lucy had come.

"Might see you later then, if Jerry's back," Tobias said loudly.

"Right you are," replied one of the others. Joe shuddered. Those three words were enough to confirm exactly what he'd feared: this was John Jackson, one of the footmen from Lucy's time in Bristol. The third man remained silent, but Joe was ready to bet it would be Metcalfe, the other Bristol footman. That was nearly as bad as finding Jackson here, since Metcalfe always went along with everything Jackson said.

Jackson dropped his voice again. "Don't forget to see Penrose before your papers come. We don't want you getting called up for the wrong side!"

"I won't," Tobias muttered.

The back of Joe's neck prickled. As though it wasn't bad enough, finding these three together again, it sounded as though they were plotting something, just like before! They might be in a different world now, but that wouldn't have changed the kind of men they were. These were men who'd thought nothing of selling innocent people into slavery, even children!

"Quick!" hissed Lucy. "They're leaving. We should have been further down the street." She shoved the bike along the road a few paces. It rasped very obviously. She stopped and knelt down next to it. "It's just as well we're nearly there," she said, in a voice that rang out shrilly in the evening air. "I thought it was only a puncture, but there's a nail."

Joe bent and pretended to look. "Can you fix it?" he asked, playing along. His tone sounded forced and unconvincing, like a bad actor.

"I think we've got an old tyre at home," Lucy replied. "We should be able to patch it up. Come on." She stood up.

Joe looked around. Tobias was on the opposite side of the road now, walking swiftly away. He didn't seem to have seen them. Even if he had, Joe knew Tobias wouldn't have recognised him from the past.

Being a stranger in each new world did have some advantages.

"Where are the other two?" he whispered.

"Gone the other way." Lucy pushed the bike onwards along the street. "Tobias lives on the next road. He works for the greengrocer on the corner. I'm not sure about the others. I wondered what they were up to, that's all, coming out of the shelter when there isn't a raid. A lot of people don't use those shelters even when there is. They stink of boiled cabbage and pee, and they're freezing cold. Nobody would go inside one when it's quiet unless they were up to something they shouldn't be!"

Joe thought for a few moments, weighing up how much he could safely say. He knew Lucy was right, but he couldn't offer a good reason for agreeing with her.

He was saved from answering by Lucy stopping at one of the terraced houses. "This is us," she said, steering the bike through the gate and leaning it beneath the front window.

She pushed the door open. "It's only me," she called. She hung her coat on a hook with Joe's and led the way along the hall to a small kitchen at the back.

Joe halted in the doorway, looking past her. The room was warm but dreary, lit only by a few coals glowing in the small grate and a dim globe of light hanging from the ceiling. The curtains at the window were thin and didn't quite meet in the middle. Through the gap, Joe saw that the glass had been covered with black fabric.

A woman stood with her back to them, washing up in a shallow brown sink. Everything around her looked worn out, from the blotchy wooden draining board beside her to the linoleum beneath her feet. Next to the sink, two pans bubbled on the gas rings of a little white cooker. The room smelled of damp washing and overcooked vegetables, and something else similarly unpleasant.

The woman turned round. "Here you are at last, Lucy. We were starting to wonder where you'd got to!"

Joe was perplexed. Since this was Lucy's house, he'd assumed the woman would be her mother, Ellen. She wasn't. All the same, he thought he knew her, though he couldn't quite place her. At least she wasn't cross with Lucy for being late. If this had been him, his mother would have been snappy with worry.

"I burst one of the bicycle tyres in a pothole," Lucy said.

"It was my fault." Joe stepped forward. "I walked out in front of her. I'm really sorry."

"Is that what she brought you back here for, to say sorry?" the woman asked him. "Or are you going to fix the bike?"

Joe reddened. "I can try," he said, "though I haven't had much practice at that sort of thing."

The woman laughed. "I'm only teasing. That

sounds like my husband coming in now. I'm sure he and Peter can do it between them."

Joe turned. The front door had opened again. In the hall stood a handsome black man.

Joe blinked. This was someone he definitely knew: Amos, the freed slave from Bristol. He beamed. Over the past few months, he'd found himself thinking of Amos surprisingly often. He'd been one of the most quietly self-controlled people Joe had ever met, yet at the same time, one of the most impressive.

Even so, Joe felt a spark of surprise that Amos should be married to this woman. Had it been common for people of different races to marry in Britain in 1940? He doubted it. Presumably, Amos *was* British this time, another Liverpudlian perhaps, like Lucy and the woman. Or might he be American? There had been American soldiers in Britain in World War Two, Joe remembered, but he was sure they'd come later on.

All at once, his mind jumped sideways. Was it coincidence that he should see Tobias, Jackson and Amos within a few minutes of each other? Tobias and Jackson's campaign of cruelty against Amos had almost ended in catastrophe. What might their scheming mean for Amos this time? A chill ran through Joe, freezing the smile on his lips.

Amos' face changed as he watched Joe, surprise and pleasure giving way to a faint weariness.

"Go on through, Amos," said a man from beyond him. "My wife is probably in the kitchen. She does the cooking on Tuesdays – it's her night off work. My sister will be around somewhere too."

Joe stepped aside to let Amos and his companion enter the kitchen.

"Ah, this is my niece, Lucy," said the man. Lucy, this is Able Seaman Amos Harper."

"Pleased to meet you, Mr. Harper," Lucy said.

"Just plain 'Amos' is good enough for me," Amos replied. He smiled at Lucy, and her face lit up in response, as though mirroring his expression. Joe marvelled again at the way Amos did that. He'd had this gift before, of bringing warmth to a room. His voice was as deep and rich as ever, and though his English was less accented this time, it still had a distinct West Indian ring to it.

"This good lady is my wife, Jane," Lucy's uncle continued. "Amos is in the merchant navy, as you'll guess from his uniform. He's not due to leave port until Friday, and he's been missing his family. I thought I'd bring him back here for a few home comforts, and to remind him of the happy chaos he's left behind in London!"

There was the sound of feet on the stairs followed by a movement in the hallway behind the two men. "I don't know what you mean by 'chaos', Tom!" Lucy's mother appeared at the man's side. She dug him in the ribs as she squeezed past into the kitchen, which was starting to feel crowded.

"This is my sister, Ellen," Tom said to Amos.

Joe felt relief rise in him. With Ellen here as well as Lucy, he was definitely in the right place.

"She's kindly taken us in while our house is repaired. We were bombed out," Tom added. "I can't remember if I said."

As Tom introduced Amos to Ellen, Joe searched through his memory. Lucy's Uncle Tom and Aunt Jane – he knew he'd met them both in the past, but not recently. He glanced across at Jane, who'd dried her hands on her apron and was shaking Amos' hand. Her hair was neatly curled and pinned back from her face in the same style as Ellen's, but the dress beneath her apron was as drab as everyone else's clothes. Joe felt sure she'd been more impressive when he'd met her before.

Then he had it! Jane had been the lady of the castle at Old Wardour, and her husband was Sir Thomas. No wonder it had taken him a while to recognise them! Back then, they'd been rich and powerful, living very differently to this. That would be over a year and a half ago, almost four hundred years if he was counting historically! He smiled to himself.

Silence fell. Joe realised with a jolt that everyone was waiting for him to speak. He looked swiftly from face to face to find Ellen's gaze fixed on him.

"I'm Joe Hopkins, Mrs Lucas," he said, hoping he'd guessed her question correctly. "I'm afraid I knocked Lucy off her bike this evening by accident."

"Oh dear." Ellen looked at her daughter and then back at Joe. "Were you hurt, either of you?"

"No," Lucy answered, "but Joe came back with me because he needs somewhere to stay, for tonight at least. He's got relatives in Liverpool, but he hasn't been able to trace them yet. He was evacuated from London to north Wales, to live with a horrible man and his wife, and he's run away. Is it alright if he stays with us?"

"Of course! Poor boy!" Ellen hesitated for a moment, then said awkwardly, "You don't happen to have your ration book, do you, Joe? We can make you up a bed on the floor for as long as you need, but it won't be easy to stretch our food rations for more than a day or two."

Joe shook his head. "I don't have my identity card either," he said, remembering the man outside the football ground. "The people I was staying with took them both away."

"Oh goodness!" Ellen bit her lip. "That's a bit more serious. You're supposed to be able to prove who you are at any time."

"He's clearly a spy!" Lucy's Aunt Jane said. Seeing Joe's confusion, she chuckled. "There are spies everywhere, or so you'd think. Nearly every week someone claims to have seen a nun with hairy legs under her habit!"

"What?" Joe was bewildered.

"German parachutists in disguise!"

"I shouldn't worry," Tom said. "As long as you keep out of mischief, the chances are nobody'll even ask to see your ID."

Joe swallowed. That might not be as easy as it sounded. After his experience this evening outside Anfield, being in the wrong place at the wrong time could be enough to land him in hot water.

"Your uncle and aunt will be able to help you when you find them, I expect," Ellen said. "In the meantime, we'll feed you as best we can."

Amos cleared his throat. "I brought something to help out," he said diffidently. From the pocket of his uniform, he brought out two small boxes. Joe was puzzled. Both had the word 'cigarettes' on them. Surely Amos didn't think people would eat those!

Ellen took them gratefully from him, however. "That's very thoughtful of you," she said. "We've got several neighbours who'll gladly exchange some of their rations for these. You probably know, cigarettes are in short supply lately."

Amos nodded. "I always pick up what I can before the convoy leaves Nova Scotia. I have something the children might like, too." From another pocket, he brought out a packet wrapped in brown paper and handed it to Lucy.

"Chocolate!" she cried as she unwrapped it. It wasn't a very large bar, Joe saw, only four squares wide by about ten long. Lucy flung her arms around Amos, who glowed with delight. "We haven't had this much chocolate in months!" she cried.

"You know how to make sure you get a good welcome!" laughed her uncle. "Any time you're in Liverpool, this door will be open!"

"He would have been just as welcome without it," Ellen said reproachfully.

"Besides," Jane added, "he might not want to come again after tonight's supper. It's Lord Woolton Pie again."

Tom groaned theatrically.

"What's Lord Woolton Pie?" Amos asked.

"Steak and kidney pie without the steak and kidney," Tom said, "or the pie. Maybe you haven't had it on the ships yet. The Minister for Food has been all over the news, pretending he's proud as punch to have such a delicious recipe named after him."

"I'm sure he's right," Amos said gallantly.

"It's more filling than delicious," Jane said, pulling a face. "Turnips, swede, carrots, potatoes, and potato pastry on the top."

"It sounds very … healthy." Amos grinned. "But can you spare enough for me as well as young Joe here?"

"You can have mine," Tom said promptly.

"And mine!" came a voice from the hall.

A boy appeared in the kitchen doorway. His fair hair was cut short at the back and sides in a style Joe had seen in films and photos from the wartime. He was a good deal taller than he'd been before, but Joe recognised him at once as Lucy's brother, Peter.

So here was all of Lucy's family now, except for her father. There were far fewer of them than there used to be, but after his conversations with Lucy in the last two worlds, Joe guessed this might be how it was now: the Lucases had become an ordinary two-child family, rather than a family scarred over and over by infant deaths.

"What have you done to my bike, Lucy?" Peter was asking indignantly. "The front wheel's bent and the tyre is completely flat! I wouldn't have lent it to you if I'd known you were going to wreck it!"

"Manners please, Peter," Ellen chided him. "Don't you see we have guests? This is Amos Harper, a friend of your uncle's, and Joe Hopkins, who came back with Lucy and will be staying with us. This is my son, Peter."

Peter nodded pleasantly to Amos and Joe. Then he frowned at Lucy again. "What happened?"

"I hit a pothole."

"Very bad luck," Tom said. As Joe opened his mouth to apologise for a fourth time, Lucy's uncle winked at him. "I'll help you mend it, Peter," he said. "Let's do it now, shall we, before we eat, so the glue has a chance to set?"

"Alright." Peter scowled at Lucy. "I think there's an old tyre in the loft. I'll go and see." He stumped back out to the hall with Tom behind him.

Lucy turned to Amos. She still had the chocolate

bar clutched in her hand, but she seemed to have forgotten about it. "Was that you and Uncle Tom coming along the street behind us?"

Amos nodded. "We saw you with the bike."

"Did you see the men by the air raid shelter?"

"Two of them?"

"Three."

"Two went past us on the other side of the road. Why?"

"You didn't happen to recognise them, did you? I thought if they were from the docks, you might know them."

Amos considered her question. "It was very dark," he said. "I'm not sure."

Joe fidgeted in frustration. If only he could tell Lucy and Amos what he knew! But how could he explain himself?

"One of the voices might have been familiar," Amos said. "Not the first one I heard, the second."

Joe chewed his tongue. "Could he have been called Jackson, or something like that?" he said, trying to sound tentative.

Lucy looked at him in surprise. "What makes you say that?"

"I thought I heard one of the others say it," Joe lied. "And something that sounded like Metcalfe? Do those names mean anything to you?"

He saw alertness appear in Amos' eyes.

"Your hearing is a lot better than mine," Lucy

said. "I didn't hear anything like that. The only name I caught was Penrose, but it didn't sound like he was one of them."

"He wasn't," Joe said, remembering the fisherman he'd known by that name. It would be good to meet George Penrose again here, with his twinkling eyes and his bushy, red beard. Suddenly, another connection clicked into place in Joe's brain. Long ago, there had been a Viking with the same fiery hair and the same jovial manner. Joe didn't think he'd ever known his name, but that had to have been George! He was amazed he hadn't realised before.

Lucy was looking at him curiously. "You sound very certain."

Joe hesitated. He'd forgotten what he'd just said.

"George Penrose is in charge of the wages and contracts down at the docks," Ellen interrupted. "He hires men when they're needed."

Lucy rubbed her temple thoughtfully.

"Jackson and Metcalfe, though –" Amos said. "You know, I have seen two men by those names. That could well have been them. But what on earth were they doing here? They're up to no good, I'll be bound."

4

"You know, that's exactly what I thought!" Lucy exclaimed.

So did I, Joe added silently. He didn't know whether to feel glad or worried to have his suspicions confirmed like this. "Why do you say that?" he asked.

Amos seemed to be gathering his thoughts. After a few moments, he said, "Last time I was in port here, a few weeks ago, I overheard two men talking about the cargo of my ship. I can't remember exactly what they said, but there was something shifty about them. I asked someone who they were. He told me their names were John Jackson and Walter Metcalfe."

"What did you think they were doing?"

"I don't know. I saw them together a few times, skulking, it looked like. So I started asking around. It turns out there's been a lot going missing down there. Almost every ship that arrives or leaves has less cargo than it should. Things are disappearing right under the noses of the port authorities."

"For the black market, you mean?" Ellen looked round, a bundle of cutlery in one hand and a folded tablecloth in the other.

"Some of it," Amos said. "Meat, for sure – there was a whole truck of lamb carcasses that vanished."

To Joe's surprise, Jane burst out laughing. "That's hardly a secret! There are days you take your life in your hands if you walk down the road next to the dock wall."

"Why?" Joe gaped at her.

"All the frozen meat being flung over! A leg of lamb can be enough to kill you!" She caught sight of her sister-in-law's face. "I don't know why you look so shocked, Ellen. You must know it happens! I can think of half a dozen shops between here and Walton where they sell all kinds of things under the counter, no ration book, no questions asked."

"Do you buy things off the black market, then?" Lucy asked her, wide-eyed.

"Chance would be a fine thing!" Jane grinned. "We can't afford it. But there are plenty who can and do."

"And plenty who feather their own nests along the way," Amos said with a frown. "I asked the man in charge of loading and unloading, a man called Stanford, if he knew anything about it."

"What did he say?"

All eyes were on Amos, but the sailor's gaze slid away. "I couldn't repeat it in polite company," he replied. "The message was clear enough: that I should go back to where I came from – and he didn't mean London – and keep my nose out of things that had nothing to do with me."

"That's so rude," Lucy cried, "and so unfair! It has everything to do with you, doesn't it? My father says if it weren't for men like you, risking your lives to bring food across the Atlantic, the country would starve and Germany would win the war!"

Amos gave her a fleeting smile. "I didn't care about the insult. Those things have been said to me by white men all my life. But I did care about the cargo disappearing. Far too much of it doesn't get here in the first place – on that convoy, the one I heard Jackson talking about, we'd lost twelve ships of the fifty that set out from Nova Scotia." He shook his head slowly. "Good men were drowned, a lot of them, men I'd sailed with, men I knew. Every one of them was someone's son, maybe someone's sweetheart or husband, or a father like me."

It was quiet in the kitchen for a moment.

Amos' eyebrows drew together. "You know what they call the fleets of U-Boats, the German submarines? Wolfpacks, because of the way they hunt us across the Atlantic. They're out there waiting for us night and day. They know we have to keep going. When they find a convoy, they close in, like a pack of wolves. They even call them 'kills', the ships they sink, and they pick off as many as they can."

"Like the *City of Benares*," Lucy said.

49

There was such suppressed feeling in her voice that Joe couldn't help but ask, "What's that?"

"Did you not hear?" Ellen was astonished. "It was all over the news! The *City of Benares* was a ship that was sunk by German submarines just a few days out of Liverpool. There were ninety children on board being sent away to safety in Canada. The U-Boats torpedoed her. Almost all of the children died, including a girl we knew."

Amos nodded. "They'll stop at nothing," he said. "If I let myself think about it, I'd be too scared to go on. I have to think about *why* we're doing it − for Britain, for the war effort. That's why it makes me sick to think of the likes of Stanford, safe on dry land, taking money to look the other way. I don't believe it's just petty theft either, not just food."

"Why? What else is on the ships?"

"Military supplies, aircraft parts, in some of the convoys there are whole aeroplanes on their way to RAF Speke to be put together. The black market is one thing, but interfering with cargoes like that would be sabotage."

"Is that what you think is happening?" Joe asked. The room was very still again.

Then Amos shrugged. "I don't know. Even if I did, nobody will listen to me."

"You should tell my husband," Ellen said. "He's a rigger down at the docks. What you're talking about isn't his line, but he's well respected. He's on late shift this week, so he might still be down there if you're going back later. His name is William Lucas."

"Thank you." Amos nodded solemnly. "I'll find him."

There was a lot to take in, Joe thought later that evening: all the many little things that made Lucy's new world different from his own, but also everything Amos had said as well. He turned over on the bed Ellen had made up for him on the floor of Peter and Lucy's room. It wasn't a proper mattress, just a blanket she'd folded over, and it wasn't very comfortable. She'd lent him some pyjamas, but he'd had to put his jumper back on over them to stop himself shivering under the second blanket.

Was Amos right, he wondered. Was Jackson stealing supplies from the ships and passing them on to Tobias to sell on the black market? That might well have been what they were discussing in the air raid shelter. Lucy had said Tobias worked for the greengrocer, so it was probably easy enough for him to find customers for stolen goods and split the money with Jackson.

Stanford was plainly taking his cut as well, as payment for overlooking the thefts. That didn't surprise Joe. This was almost certainly the same Stanford who'd been the pompous constable in Bristol. He might have been on the right side of the law then, but he'd nearly allowed the *Isabella* to sail before its human cargo could be rescued, just because Lucy's father didn't have the right paperwork. It was clear that Stanford considered himself more important than whoever he worked for. In this world, that might have a very different result.

Where George Penrose fitted in, on the other hand, Joe couldn't think. The Cornishman had been kind and decent. True, he'd been from a family of smugglers, and happy enough to fish out barrels washed in from the wreck of Joe's ship, even though they didn't belong to him. But Joe couldn't imagine him having a part in anything that would damage Britain's chances of defeating Germany. Come to that, would any of these men go as far as stealing military supplies in order to help the enemy?

As he pondered this question, it occurred to him that he hadn't yet come across a single person here that he didn't already know, except for the man outside Anfield. Even he had seemed familiar. With a start, Joe realised! That had been Epistolio, the Roman slave who'd tried to teach him to write! That was why he'd had the sense of being told off by him before.

How extraordinary that he knew every single person in this world already, and even every person they'd mentioned! Who else was going to pop up here? Throughout his visits to the past, the number of people who'd appeared more than once had grown steadily: Miss Waters had been there three times, and her father twice; Morley had reappeared, and so had Mary Stanton, and Harry, Hannah, and Samuel Coles. Until now, there had been others like Epistolio, who he'd only come across once. Were they too going to turn up here? What about all the new faces from Porthkellow? What about Lady Poston and Thomas Carraway?

All at once, Joe was filled with dread. He closed his eyes in the darkness and tried to remember methodically everyone he'd met with Lucy. All the while though, miserable certainty was taking shape inside him. In Cornwall this summer, he'd feared that finding so many familiar people in one place might be the curtain call, the line-up of all the characters for one final appearance. He'd been wrong then. This time, he knew he was not. This simply had to be the end of his time in the past! After all, there was almost no history left to come between now and his own world, less than eighty years. This must be the last chapter, the last time he would be with Lucy!

A small cry of despair escaped him.

"Are you alright?" Lucy asked softly.

Joe pulled the blanket over his head. He didn't trust himself to speak. "Mmmm," he mumbled, blinking furiously.

"Did you want to talk about it, whatever it is?"

"No." Joe's voice came out thick. If only he *could* talk about it. But he could never tell anyone about this. Even Lucy wouldn't understand, although she was at the heart of it.

He held his breath to calm himself. They were here together now, that was the important thing. He

53

mustn't spoil the time he had left by dreading the end of it. He screwed his eyes shut more tightly to block out the memories that his brain was sending to the surface, of all the goodbyes he had said to Lucy. The worst of it was that each time he'd left her, he'd cared more, missed her more. How would he bear the very last time? He choked.

He awoke the next morning determined to put all thought of the previous night out of his mind and make the most of his time here.

Breakfast was in the front room, which Ellen called the parlour, and looked to be an oddly formal affair compared to the ease of the supper they'd eaten in here the evening before. The Lord Woolton pie had been filling, just as Jane had promised, and very far from delicious, just as she had warned; but the company had been so light-hearted that Joe would have been happy for the meal to go on and on.

Ellen and Lucy's tiredness had been obvious, however, and even Tom's patter of jokes and stories had begun to falter by nine o'clock. From one or two remarks, Joe guessed that the air raids of the last few months had been exhausting, especially since everyone had to get up and get on as usual the next morning. What was remarkable, he thought, was that he should have to piece this together from so few comments. It was hard to imagine people in his own time complaining so little about so much.

Lucy's father, William, was at the breakfast table

when Joe came down. Joe wondered what time he'd come in the night before. Presumably, there hadn't been an air raid – from what he remembered from bits of black and white film, it wasn't likely he'd have slept through one.

William introduced himself politely to Joe, without any sign of curiosity about where he'd come from, before going back to his newspaper. He was sitting at the head of the table which had been laid with a full set of cutlery and crockery on a fresh tablecloth. Lucy and Peter sat down opposite one another and Ellen sat at the other end, pouring tea and spreading slices of heavy wholemeal bread with the thinnest smear of butter and so little jam that the colour was all but invisible. Joe took the chair beside Lucy, and began to eat.

He was still struggling through his helping by the time Peter and William left for work. Lucy's brother was apprenticed to a shipwright down at the docks, Ellen explained, following in William's footsteps, as William had followed his own father. She didn't elaborate further about what he did all day, or what Lucy's Aunt Jane and Uncle Tom did, though they'd apparently left for work much earlier. It didn't really matter, Joe thought, as long as he was allowed to spend the day with Lucy.

While he drank his tea, he listened to the conversation, trying to pick up clues about what she would be doing today. It sounded as though she still went to lessons sometimes, which was better than being sent out to work like last time. He hoped she was getting a proper education now. In past worlds where her family had been rich, she'd had a tutor or a governess, but they'd only taught her the most basic reading and writing skills, and spent the rest of the time on things like painting and dancing. She'd never learned anything useful, as far as he could see. Perhaps that had changed finally.

As if sensing his effort to work this out, Ellen said, "Lucy got a scholarship to the girls' grammar school last year." There was unmistakable pride in her voice. "She's the first in our family to get to grammar school. She worked really hard for it." She smiled at her daughter.

"That's terrific!" Joe said, forcing a smile of his own. Only it wasn't terrific. He'd thought there was no school, after what the Epistolio man had said. If there was, and she was at an all-girls' school, he wouldn't be able to go with her! He was gripped again by the sense of time running out.

"Mind you, she hasn't had much out of it so far," Ellen went on regretfully. "The whole school was evacuated with two of the teachers when she started last September. Most of the girls came home after a few weeks, but by then the rest of the staff had been called up, to the forces or for war work. The building's been taken over by the war office as well. Goodness knows what they're doing in there! So all she has is two or three hours every other afternoon, at the house of one or another of the girls."

"That was where I was coming back from yesterday, when I crashed into you," Lucy said.

Joe nodded, trying not to let his relief show.

"It's a beautiful house Dorothy's parents have," she added. "It's really big, with a piano in the parlour. They've got their own Anderson shelter in the garden too, and an indoor bathroom."

Joe bit back a smile at the wistfulness in these last words. This house had a privy in the back yard like the cottage in Porthkellow, though at least here you could pull a chain to flush it. He guessed that bathing here was pretty much like Cornwall too – he'd seen a small tin bath hanging up when he went out.

Ellen said sharply. "That's very nice for Dorothy, but don't you forget we've plenty to be grateful for! We've all got shoes on our feet, and we don't have to share our privy with half the street. There are a lot of families who envy us just like you envy her." She changed the subject. "You don't have lessons today, do you?"

"No," Lucy said meekly. "It's my turn to do the shopping, isn't it? Do you want to come, Joe?"

"Alright," Joe agreed.

"And of course you need to trace your uncle."

"What?" For a split second, Joe thought she was talking about Uncle Nick. Then he remembered. "Oh, yes, of course."

Lucy frowned slightly. "We could walk down to the General Post Office in the city centre. They might have the information."

He nodded.

"I'm sure you can't wait to be with your own family again, after everything you've been through!"

"Absolutely!" Joe lied.

5

Joe didn't expect the shopping expedition to be much fun, but at least it was a way of spending time with Lucy, and being able to talk to her without Ellen or the others around. He only wished he'd already managed to tell her where he'd really come from; he would have to be very careful about what he said, and the questions he asked, since she didn't know the truth.

He wondered with a sinking feeling what she would think this time when he told her. He was fairly certain that people eighty years ago hadn't been anywhere near as superstitious as in earlier times. His own grandparents had lived through the Second World War, though they'd probably been a bit younger than Lucy. The three who were still alive back at home were old now, of course, but they were still normal, modern people with mostly sensible ideas about things. He tried to imagine meeting them when they'd been children and telling them he was from the future. It was absurd! They would never have believed it. Nor would she!

As he and Lucy set out for the shops in the weak winter sunshine, he found himself thinking nostalgically of the first few times they'd met. How simple it had been back then! She'd suggested herself that he might be an evil spirit when she first saw him in Roman Britain. Even in Tudor times, over a thousand years later, she'd been quick to believe that his St. Christopher had supernatural powers. So it hadn't been difficult to convince her that he'd come from another time. It wouldn't be like that at all here. In fact, there was probably no point in saying anything until he was about to prove it.

Walking along the street, Joe turned his mind deliberately back to the present moment. This outing might be more interesting than he'd thought. For sure, the shops were unlikely to be exotic like the market in Viking Jorvik had been, with its animal skins and silks, and its swords and axes. But he'd found the Victorian pharmacy curiously different, and even though he was now closer to his own time, buying things in wartime Britain was bound to be quite unlike supermarket shopping.

In this, he was correct: each of the shops he visited with Lucy sold something different, and not one of them was big enough to hold more than five or six customers. As a result, queues snaked out along the street from every shop doorway as people stood patiently with their baskets at their feet. Waiting with

Lucy outside the bakery, Joe soon started to get cold in his shorts and thin coat. Yet after ten minutes queuing, she only bought a single loaf.

The queue for the butcher was even longer. Joe was bored and irritable by the time she finally got to the counter and handed over the family's ration books. He assumed she felt the same, so he was taken aback to see her give the butcher her sweetest smile.

"I was wondering if you could let me have this week's bacon ration for my cousin, Joe," she said, putting her head on one side. "We haven't got his ration book at the moment. His parents sent him up here from London to stay with us, but the train was bombed. All his luggage was destroyed!" She gave Joe's arm a squeeze as though to comfort him. "Ma's going to try and stretch the food we have until his new ration book arrives, but it's so hard!" She looked up at the man behind the counter from beneath her eyelashes.

"You know very well I shouldn't, Lucy," the butcher said gruffly, cutting out the stamps from the ration books, "but we don't want you going hungry." He slipped an extra rasher of bacon into the paper package. Joe wondered if he'd misheard or misunderstood. Was a single rasher of bacon all he was allowed for the week?

"I daresay his book will come through soon enough," the butcher was saying. "Then you can bring it here to register. Do you want anything else?"

"Ma asked for a sheep's head if you have one."

Joe shivered with silent revulsion. Imagine finding a sheep's eyeballs on your plate! Fortunately, the butcher shook his head. "All gone. We've got some rabbit come in this morning, though. That makes a good stew."

"No, thank you," Lucy said. "She told me to get tripe otherwise, please."

The butcher handed the ration books back and moved along the counter. He brought out some flappy pieces of something pale yellow, covered in tiny blobs like goose bumps. Joe tried not to stare. This looked as disgusting as the sheep's head would have been, although he couldn't guess what animal it came from, nor which bit it was. It might be better not to know anyway, since knowing wouldn't save him from having to eat it later on. He waited to see if she was going to buy any other horror, but she paid and led the way out of the shop.

"You didn't need the ration books for the tripe?" he asked, when they were outside again.

"No, offal's off ration, which is good. We've always eaten quite a bit of it because it's cheap. My father's favourite food is liver and onions, so he can still have that."

"I can't believe you told the butcher such a whopping lie about my ration book!" Joe said.

Lucy grinned. "I could have told him the truth about it being in Wales, but I didn't think he'd take pity on you the same as if you'd escaped falling bombs!"

Joe had to agree. He'd been slightly shocked to hear her invent something so outrageously untrue, but it was actually a smaller lie than the one he'd told her. At least she genuinely believed he'd come from London and his ration book was somewhere else, whereas he knew that neither of those things was true.

"Look at that queue outside the greengrocers!" Lucy said. "Come on, we'll go there next." She hurried along the street to join the back of a particularly long line of people.

"Why did you do that?" Joe said, catching up with her. "Couldn't we go and do the rest of the shopping first and come back when the queue's died down?"

She furrowed her brow. "You're obviously new to this. A queue this long means there's something unusual that'll be worth getting."

"What if it's something you really don't want, like – I don't know – jellied eels?"

Lucy laughed. "It's a greengrocer! They only sell fruit and veg. But even if it was something we didn't want, we'd get it anyway and then swap it with a neighbour for something else. Things that people think are worth a long wait are good to swap."

She tapped the shoulder of the woman in front of them. "What have they got in?"

The woman turned round. "Oranges and grapefruit, I heard."

"There!" Lucy said to Joe.

"What do you mean, 'there'? You're happy to stand for half an hour for some oranges?"

"We might not even get them," Lucy said. "They might be gone by the time we get to the front. When did you last have an orange, though?"

Joe was wondering how to answer when he saw that Lucy wasn't expecting him to. She had tipped the money out of her purse and was counting it anxiously. "They might be too expensive," she said. "We still need to get butter from the dairy, and Ma wants a few things from the grocer."

"Won't the ration books cover some of it?"

She looked up, surprised. "Of course not. You still have to pay. Just because you have enough coupons doesn't mean the thing is free. The ration books are there to stop you buying more than your fair share."

Joe scratched his head. He'd always assumed that you handed over the stamps in the ration book in exchange for the goods, like vouchers.

"Ma got some extra sugar coupons a while back from one of the dockworkers my father knows," Lucy said. "They have seven children, so they're allowed a lot more sugar than we are, but they didn't have the money to buy it, so Ma paid them for the coupons and made jam with the extra sugar she got."

Joe thought of the thin layer of red across his toast this morning. That jam was clearly going to last a long time.

They stood together in silence for a while, each of them lost in thought. Gradually, the women and girls moved on ahead of them. It occurred to Joe that he was the only boy he'd seen queuing for the shops, except for much younger children holding their mothers' hands. There were no men either, except behind the counters, and they were all older. The younger ones must be away fighting in the war, he guessed. So why hadn't Metcalfe and Jackson been sent away? They must surely be the right age to be soldiers, and Tobias couldn't be far off either.

"You know, when we were eavesdropping next to the shelter last night," he said, "one of the men said something to Tobias that I didn't understand, about not being called up for the wrong side. Did you hear that?"

Lucy nodded. "That was just before they left, wasn't it, when they mentioned going to see Penrose?"

"That's right. What do you think they meant?"

"They were talking about Tobias' papers coming. He must be about to turn eighteen, so he'll be called up to go and fight, unless he's a conchie, which I doubt!"

"What's a conchie?"

Lucy looked at him. "I can't believe how out of the war you've been over there in the wilds of Wales!"

Joe flinched inwardly. "Like I said, the farm was a long way from the village," he mumbled.

"Didn't you go to school, though? Didn't you

65

hear the other kids talking about the war? Or the teachers? Didn't the man and his wife listen to the news on the wireless?"

Joe shook his head. "They didn't have a radio – I mean, a wireless – and they didn't let me go to school."

Lucy tutted. "You really were unlucky! A conchie is a conscientious objector," she went on, "someone who refuses to fight on principle."

"Couldn't anyone say they object, if they don't feel like going?" Joe asked.

"They could," she agreed. "Some do. But the authorities don't let you off just like that. You have to go to a tribunal and explain your reasons, and they have to be really strong moral or religious reasons. You can't just say you'd rather not. If they don't believe you, they'll send you off anyway, the same as everyone else. And even if they do believe that you won't kill another person come what may, they'll still allocate you some sort of war work."

"Isn't that better than fighting?"

"It might be – sometimes they send people to work on the land. But sometimes it's something like driving ambulances on the battlefield, or bomb disposal. It can be just as dangerous as it is for the troops fighting.

"Anyway, I don't suppose Tobias is a conchie, and his friends won't be either. If they work down at the docks where Amos saw them, they've probably got jobs that are exempt from call-up. A lot of jobs down there are, because the ships have to keep sailing. It counts towards the war effort just keeping the docks working, especially when they get bombed so often. The ships that get damaged by the submarines have to be repaired too, and new ships have to be built to replace the ones that have been sunk. That's enough work to keep plenty of younger men busy, even with all the older ones as well."

"Didn't you say Tobias worked for a greengrocer, though?" Joe said.

"That's right. We'll see him when we get to the front of this line."

Joe grimaced. There was no situation in which he wanted to meet Tobias, even if he was just behind a shop counter.

"What's that face for?" Lucy asked in surprise. "I'd be the first to say he isn't exactly charming, but you've never met him!"

Joe ignored the question. "So he wouldn't be exempt, would he?" he pressed on. "You just said he's going to be called up to fight."

"I should think so, unless he changes job."

"But that still doesn't explain what they meant about being called up for the wrong side, does it?"

"No," Lucy said. She stepped in through the doorway of the shop as someone left. "Look, it won't be long 'til we're at the front. Shall we ask him?"

"No!" The word came out more sharply than Joe intended. "I mean, I don't think that's a good idea."

Lucy raised her eyebrows. "I was only joking."

They moved forward another place as the woman at the front completed her purchases. A man with a neat white moustache called the next person to the counter, while Tobias continued to serve his customer.

Joe studied him, making the most of the opportunity to have a really good look. It had been a long time since he'd been able to: several of their more recent confrontations had taken place in the half-light, and on the last two occasions, Joe had been too preoccupied with the gun in Tobias' hand to focus on anything else.

He had to admit now that with a different expression, Tobias would have been startlingly handsome. There was a coppery glint to his hair which caught the light where it swept back in waves from his temples. His high cheekbones and dark eyes would have been enough to send half the girls in Joe's class into fits of giggling adoration, and he was broad shouldered and strong. Yet the emotion that radiated from the face made it ugly: there was an expression of contempt, even loathing, for everyone around him.

Tobias looked up and caught Joe's eye. Joe switched his gaze at once to the older man, and realised suddenly that this was Mr. Peekes, the Tudor gatekeeper and Lucy's Cornish neighbour. He hoped Mr. Peekes would serve Lucy rather than Tobias.

When at last they were at the front of the line

however, it was Tobias who stood before them.

"What can I get you, Miss?" he asked Lucy. Though the question was polite, the tone was insolent.

Lucy pretended not to notice. "How much are the oranges and grapefruit, please?"

"Grapefruit are all gone. We're down to the last dozen oranges at threepence each," Tobias said.

Lucy drew breath. "That's three times what they were last year!"

"Don't you know there's a war on?" retorted Tobias.

Lucy tipped her money into her hand again, and seemed to be adding up in her head.

"Where did they come from?" Joe asked boldly.

"Off a ship, of course," Tobias replied with a curl of the lip. "Where else?" He turned to Lucy again. "Do you want any or not? They'll soon be gone."

"I'll take three," Lucy said.

"Ration books!" snapped Tobias.

Lucy handed them over.

"Only this one," he said, holding up the blue one with Lucy's name on. "Oranges are reserved for children and pregnant women only."

Lucy glanced sidelong at Joe, but seemed to decide against arguing. It was clear that Tobias wouldn't give her anything for Joe without a ration book.

"One orange at threepence, and you can have an extra one for sixpence," Tobias offered.

Lucy shook her head. Her cheeks flushed.

"Anything else?"

"Two cabbages, please." She held out her basket for Tobias to put them in, along with some scoops of potatoes, carrots and turnips which he tipped in on top of the orange.

"That was horrible!" she exploded, when they were outside on the pavement afterwards. "The price of those oranges! Sixpence for an extra one – that's daylight robbery! I'm sure he short-changed me as well!"

"I was wondering if the oranges were stolen," Joe said. "That could have been just the sort of thing Tobias was talking to those other men about last night. I'm surprised Mr. Peekes allows it."

Lucy paused in the middle of tucking her purse away and looked at Joe. "How do you know his name?"

Joe gulped. He looked back at the shop. "Peekes Greengrocer – it's above the door," he said, grateful to be able to cover his tracks. "What's next then? Have we nearly finished?"

"Only the dairy and the grocers left," Lucy said. She heaved the basket onto her arm. "Then we'll drop this lot off at home and go out to find your uncle, okay?"

"Okay," Joe agreed. It was the first time he'd ever heard her use that word. The modernness of it jarred. It was the same thing he'd been thinking before:

how close this world was to his own.

He shoved the thought firmly away and turned his mind to the business of his non-existent uncle. Hopefully, the queues for the remaining shops would be nice and long. He needed time to work out what he was going to do.

6

Joe carried the basket home for Lucy. They had queued for almost another half an hour for a pat of butter from the dairy, and some candles and blue paper screws of tea and sugar from the general store. The quantities they'd bought had been quite small though, so the only heavy things in the basket were the vegetables. Joe noticed the word Co-operative over the door of the last shop and wondered whether it was the same as the Co-op at the end of his own street. Even if it was, Lucy still had to wait for the shopkeeper to weigh out her purchases. There was no helping yourself here.

As they walked back, Joe wondered gloomily if they would have to go shopping again tomorrow for more food. Even though it had taken half the morning, he couldn't believe they'd got enough to feed a full household for more than a day or two on anything other than root vegetables. He hadn't seen a fridge in the kitchen, he realised, or a freezer either. Perhaps people had to shop several times a week for small amounts, especially for food that would go off – except that Lucy had bought all the bacon and butter they were allowed for the next seven days, hadn't she?

"Why don't you write to your mother before dinner?" she suggested, as he put the shopping basket down on the kitchen table. It was quiet in the house. Although the front door had been unlocked, Ellen seemed to be out like everyone else. Joe couldn't remember what she'd said she was doing today. Something to do with volunteering.

"I know I said we'd walk down to the General Post Office on Victoria Street," Lucy went on. "I was thinking we'd look in their telephone directories for your uncle's address. But the shopping took such a long time this morning and it's two miles each way to the GPO. It might be a waste of time anyway – if your uncle doesn't have a telephone, he won't be listed. That's how it would be if you tried to look us up. You wouldn't find us, or any of our neighbours either."

Joe nodded. He was entirely happy to give up on tracing imaginary relatives. If he followed Lucy's suggestion and posted a letter, Ellen would hopefully be happy for him to stay until a reply arrived. Since that would never happen, it was a much better solution.

He took the fountain pen and paper Lucy gave him and sat down at the kitchen table while Lucy moved round, putting the shopping away. The tripe and bacon went into a wooden cupboard with a wire mesh over the door, Joe noticed, and she put the butter under a cloth on a stone slab.

"Your handwriting is strange," she said, glancing over his shoulder as she tipped the sugar into a bowl. "Don't you practise at school? Everyone I know writes the same, and it looks nothing like that."

"This is how we write down in London," Joe lied. His handwriting was a bit untidier than usual, he had to admit, because the fountain pen was rather difficult to use. Still, it was better than a quill!

"Really? I never knew it was different around the country!" She was clearly fascinated.

"Be quiet for a moment. I need to think what to write," Joe said, to stop her asking more questions.

A few minutes later, he'd scribbled a few short lines, explaining where he was and what had happened, according to the story he'd told Lucy. "What's your address here?" he asked.

"124 Benedict Street, Bootle."

Joe added this across the bottom of the letter and put it in the envelope. While Lucy went to find a stamp, he wrote his mum's name, but his dad's address on the front. He was looking at it, his head on one side, when she came back in.

"All done?" she asked, licking the back of the stamp and sticking it on for him.

"Yes, thanks." It was an odd way to have addressed the envelope, but he couldn't think of a better one. Lucy was expecting him to write to his mother, yet it would be much more difficult to explain a letter from the past to Mum than to Dad. His father would think something like that was just a bit of fun if it arrived, not that it ever would, of course.

There was a noise in the hallway and Ellen appeared, flustered and out of breath. "Sorry I wasn't back when you came in," she said. "Mrs Cleaver is so bossy. She does like to have things just so. Let me get us something to eat."

"Can I help?" Joe asked politely. He remembered a Mrs Cleaver in Lucy's last world. She'd liked things just so, too.

Ellen smiled. "You could get some coal in. The coal scuttle is in the parlour."

Joe fetched it, and carried it out to the yard. When he came back with the coal, she had cut up the orange and put three of the quarters on plates, with another quarter set aside. "I know it's only a Wednesday, but a little luxury now and then doesn't do any harm!" She beamed at Joe and Lucy.

Lunch, or dinner as Lucy had called it, was more bread and some cold mashed potato from the day before. Joe thought of the way Dad made it, golden with all the butter and milk he added. This was greyish in colour and not nearly as nice, but at least it filled his stomach.

"Mrs Cleaver gave me some apples," Ellen said, handing Joe and Lucy one each and pouring three cups of tea. "She may be an old battleaxe, but she's generous with it." She pushed the cups and saucers across the table. "Are you going to go out this afternoon? It's a nice day, and you've earned it with your shopping trip this morning."

"We could play out in the street," Lucy said. "Or I might take Joe up to Derby Park. It's got a witch's hat and jerkers," she added, looking at him.

Joe nodded. He hoped it didn't show that he had no idea what she was talking about.

As they closed the front door behind them a while later, however, she said, "We're not going to go to Derby Park actually, at least not to the park itself."

"Oh?" Joe was taken aback. "Why did you say we were?"

"Because Ma wouldn't want us to go where I'm taking you."

"Where's that, then?"

"We're going to my favourite bombsite."

Joe blinked. "You have a favourite bombsite?"

Lucy laughed at his surprise. "Bombsites are fun! You're not supposed to go into them because they might be dangerous. The walls that are left could collapse, or there could be an explosion from a broken gas pipe. But all the kids I know do it, and there are plenty of grown-ups who go and have a poke around too, when nobody's looking. You find all sorts of things in the rubble. You just have to make sure you don't get caught by one of the air raid wardens!"

Joe thought of the Epistolio man. The 'W' on his tin hat might have been for 'Warden', and he could see why you wouldn't want to get caught by him. All the same, he was glad to have the chance to indulge the curiosity he'd felt at the ruined houses he and Lucy had passed last evening. "What's special about your favourite one?"

"The house used to be huge," she replied. "It has lovely gardens too, instead of a back yard like us. There are others like it along that road, but this is the only one that's got bombed so far. Sometimes, I pretend it's where I used to live, and my parents were killed in the raid."

Joe pulled a face. "Isn't that a bit strange? Your mum and dad are really nice. I mean, they seem really nice," he added hastily, "not that I've talked to your dad properly. You'd be sad if they died."

"Of course!" Lucy grinned. "It's only pretend! I just think it would have been wonderful to live there. In the first few days after the raid, there were all kinds of weird things. The house must have had big attics, and its cellars are still half there, too. I found a tall, stuffed cat with spots and pointy ears, and there were funny old clothes in a chest, and hats, and paintings, and all sorts of other things under the dust and grit. It's mostly gone now of course, but at least there's still the garden."

"Where's it gone?"

"Tidied away," Lucy said.

"Tidied away? You mean stolen?"

Lucy shrugged. "Not exactly. Taken. There was nobody to steal it from, as far as I know. The owners were killed and they had no family. Besides, what's the good of leaving the things that survive the bombs to get destroyed by the rain? They might as well be reused."

"How do you reuse a stuffed cat?"

"No idea!" She laughed. "I found one of my best bits of shell there, too."

"Shell?"

She glanced at Joe as they walked. "Bombshell. I suppose you won't have had any raids where you were." She whistled beneath her breath. "You should be glad you weren't here a few months ago. From the twenty-eighth of August until the end of September we had raids almost every night. Maybe you heard the planes as they headed off back to Germany or wherever. I think they sometimes loop round over Wales."

Joe thought it best to agree. "That's right, I do remember."

"Well, ever since then, kids have started collecting bits of shell cases from the bombs. If you're really lucky, you can sometimes find a fin. Everyone wants one of those. We collect shrapnel too, from the ack-ack guns – you know, the anti-aircraft guns they fire at the bombers when they fly over."

"Sounds cool!" Joe said, without thinking.

"That's a funny thing to say." Lucy was puzzled. "The best chance of finding a really good bit is the morning after a raid, but they're not cool then. They're often still too hot to touch!"

"Will we find some today?"

"Maybe, though all the obvious pieces will have been collected by now. There hasn't been a raid since last Friday, and that was mostly over Great George Street. That's an hour's walk from here, not the way we're going either. Still, I can show you my collection when we get home, and Peter's. He's got some really big bits, and one with numbers on! He's traded a few to try and make a complete shell case. Everyone wants to do that, but it's pretty much impossible.

"Anyway, you never know, we might find something 'cool' in the garden. Nobody's done anything to it since September, so it's all overgrown like a jungle."

It wasn't quite Joe's idea of a jungle, he thought, as he climbed after Lucy through a gap in the fence a while later. Jungles were green and vibrant with life, whereas this place was decaying and silent. Frost had killed off the flowers but they still hung among thickets of tall, brown stalks, tilted over in different directions. The leaves of the trees lay in bedraggled rings on the ground around them, and no birds sang.

Lucy hadn't exaggerated the size of the gardens, though. As she showed him around, pointing out things she'd noticed on other visits, Joe felt like he was in a small park. There was a tall conifer which would be good to climb up inside, and knee-high lawns dotted with shrubs big enough to hide in. He could see it would be a fabulous place to come in the summer, especially if you lived in a cramped terrace like Lucy.

In the midst of it all was a wide mound of rubble. The rooms of the house must have been big to spread over such a broad area, but there was no way of working out how it had been. Stubs of walls poked out here and there, the ragged edges of the bricks already softening from the rain. A door frame stuck up, diamond-shaped now rather than rectangular, and Joe could make out a few ends of floorboards, still mostly buried in the ruin.

"A lot of the timber's been taken already," Lucy said. "People want anything that burns, especially now it's getting cold. I'm not sure there's anything much interesting left."

"I'd still like to look," Joe said.

He picked his way cautiously over the outer edge of the rubble and lifted a rough block of bricks that were mortared together. He put it carefully to one side before trying to shift a piece of wood beneath them. This had to be cleared before it could be moved. Gradually, he lifted bits of stone and twisted pipe, themselves partly buried, until the plank was free. It was rather like being down at the seashore, lifting rocks, he thought, though most of these rocks were obstructed by other rocks, and he was unlikely to find a crab!

He worked away at it for a while. Nearby, Lucy was clearing rubble from another area, making piles on the grass. A thought occurred to Joe. "What happened to the people who lived here?" he asked, straightening up. "You said they were killed. They're not underneath this lot, are they?"

Lucy looked up. "No. They got them out. I asked someone. The woman was dead already, and the man died on the way to the hospital."

"Phew!" Joe shook his head to dispel the image of a hand reaching out of the ruins towards him.

For some time, they continued picking around companionably amongst the remains of the house. Lucy had been right, there wasn't much to find. Joe uncovered a bath tap, a few nuts and bolts, a lot of nails, and some shards of coloured glass. There was a pile of broken china too.

Then he thought he saw something glint in the light. Carefully, he moved aside the pieces of smashed crockery, never taking his eyes off the spot where the thing had flashed.

At last, he had it. It was a ring, so dirty he was amazed it had caught the light at all. He rubbed it against his sleeve. It might be gold, perhaps, or very tarnished silver. There were marks engraved over part of the band in a pleasing pattern.

"Lucy!" he called. "Come and see what I've found!" He straightened up and rubbed off the rest of the grime all the way round the ring as she picked her way across to him.

"That's lovely!" she said, taking it and examining it carefully. "I said you could find interesting things here, didn't I? You never know, it might be worth quite a lot. It looks pretty old." She held it out to him.

Joe didn't take it. "Why don't you keep it?" he said.

"But it's yours. You found it. If it's valuable, you should have it."

"Maybe, but –" He hesitated. He couldn't very well tell her that he wouldn't be able to take it back into his own time with him. "I think it's for a girl or a woman," he said instead. "Try it on."

She did so. It shone on her finger. "Are you sure?" She beamed. "I do like it."

"Good. It's yours." He shifted his feet. It felt uncomfortably symbolic to be giving a ring to her.

Lucy didn't notice. "Do you want to keep digging or shall we play hide and seek?" she asked.

Joe's hands were scuffed, he realised. Now that he'd stopped burrowing, they were starting to stiffen in the cold as well. He was unlikely to find anything better than the ring either. "Alright," he agreed. He couldn't remember the last time he'd played hide and seek, but this would be the perfect place. "You've got a big advantage over me, though," he said. "You know this garden inside out."

"I've shown you most of it," she replied. "There's one other corner we haven't been, round where the tool shed is behind those trees." She pointed. "There are a lot of nettles and brambles over there, so if you go that way, mind your legs."

"Can I hide first?"

"If you like. I'll count to thirty." She covered her eyes and began.

Joe scrambled out of the ruins and set off across the garden. At the conifer, he paused, wondering whether to climb it. He didn't have long, and if the branches were still waving when she came looking, he'd be immediately obvious.

He turned away and ran through the trees in the direction she'd indicated for the tool shed. The fact that she hadn't shown him this part of the garden, along with the warnings about getting stung, suggested she didn't come over here very much. She'd probably search everywhere else first, which would give him a chance to hide himself really well.

He didn't find the tool shed straight away, but he knew he was in the right place because there was a gigantic bramble bush which had sprung up unchecked. It must have been here already before the bomb fell because there was no way it had grown this large in just a few weeks. He circled it, looking to see if there was a tunnel into the middle.

There wasn't, but behind it was indeed a small shed. Or rather, two halves of a small shed. Joe stopped. Embedded in the corrugated iron roof, splitting it apart, was a very large grey cylinder.

His eyes travelled up. The cylinder seemed to be suspended from some pieces of cord, which themselves were attached to fabric caught in the branches of a tree. He stood very still. The nose of the cylinder was only a few centimetres from the ground, dragging the tree downwards with its weight.

"Coming!"

He heard Lucy's voice distantly and opened his mouth to answer, then closed it again. Very slowly, he began to back away. How long had the bomb been there? Was it a dud? Was that why it hadn't exploded? Or had the tree broken its fall and stopped it detonating? If that was the case, it might go off at any moment, especially if something disturbed it.

"What on earth are you doing?" Lucy's voice was closer now. "That's not hiding! I can see you right across the garden!"

Without looking round, Joe stretched out his hand towards her, signalling to her to be quiet. The bomb was out of sight from where she was, hidden by the bramble bush. He didn't take his eyes off it.

"What's the matter? Is there someone there?" She ran through the long grass towards him.

"Slow down!" he hissed. It seemed as though he could feel her feet pounding against the ground. The slightest vibration might be enough to dislodge the bomb and set it off.

She halted a few paces behind him. "Oh, my goodness!" she breathed. "We need to get away from here quickly!"

7

Joe hadn't known he could glide, but that was exactly what he seemed to do now. He and Lucy moved as quietly and smoothly as possible back across the garden to the gap in the fence.

"How long do you think it's been there?" he asked when after they'd climbed back through and crossed the road. He hoped they were far enough away now to be safe if the bomb did go off. The fence was flimsy, just a few bits of board nailed up to keep people out. It wouldn't do anything to protect them if they were still within range.

"I don't know." Her voice shook a little, but her eyes were bright. "I haven't been here for a week at least. It could have been dropped during the last raid, and nobody's noticed."

"Wouldn't people in the houses over the back have seen it?"

"Maybe not. It's buried quite deep in the shed, isn't it? And the parachute and cord is all on this side of the tree."

"How far will the damage spread if it goes off?" Joe glanced nervously back towards the gap.

"I'm not sure. It was enormous, wasn't it? Must have been over eight feet long. I'd reckon it's a thousand pounder at least, maybe two thousand pounds."

Joe was momentarily baffled until he realised she was talking about the weight. He could hear from her tone that she was proud of how much she knew. All the same, it was alarming to think of the pair of them messing about in the ruins when it might have gone off at any moment.

"So what do we do?" he asked.

"Go and find the ARP post, I suppose. They'll call bomb disposal."

"What if someone else goes in while we're gone?"

Lucy looked up and down the empty street. "It's not very likely, is it?"

"Don't you think we should tell people in the houses either side?"

"We could, though I'd say it's the ones behind that are most in danger, the houses that back onto the garden. We'd be better off going to find the air-raid warden. He can deal with it. Some wardens are quite fussy about the right way of doing things, especially the day-time ones. They're often retired, older men. A lot of them fought in the last war, so they can be a bit military."

She set off swiftly along the street so that Joe had to hurry to keep up. At the junction, she looked both ways. "There's a shop down there. The post is probably in there."

"Why don't we just knock on a door and ask someone?"

"Because they'll want to know why," Lucy said. "We don't want to start a stampede. Hang on, it's there, look."

Joe followed her gaze. "Isn't that just where someone lives?"

"Why else would it have that 'ARP' sign in the front window?" She shook her head at him. "ARP: Air Raid Precautions!" She sped off along the road once more.

Joe caught her up as she knocked on the door. It opened. At once, he took a step back. The uniformed man peering down at them was Epistolio - or whatever he was called here - the same man who'd caught Joe outside the football ground. How unlucky to come face to face with him a second time, especially so far from Anfield! Joe lowered his head and hoped the man wouldn't recognise him.

"Please, Sir," Lucy said, "we've found an unexploded bomb just down the road there." She waved a hand past Joe.

"A UXB?" barked the warden. "On Breeze Hill? Where?"

"In the gardens of the bombed house." Lucy

sounded sheepish. Joe glanced up and saw her cheeks were red.

"Playing in the ruins, were you?" the warden snapped. "You know that's forbidden! You could get hurt. Sounds like you were lucky not to get killed. What kind of bomb?"

"A parachute mine, one of the really big ones."

Joe noticed Lucy didn't offer her assessment of its weight. Maybe she wasn't so confident after all.

The warden put on his tin hat with the 'W' on it, and picked up the receiver of the telephone on the hall table. "Major Eric Postlethwaite here!" he announced importantly. "We have a UXB in the Derby Park district." Postlethwaite put one hand over the mouth of the receiver. "Number 10?" he asked. "Where in the gardens is it?"

"In the back right corner. It's stuck in the roof of the shed. The parachute's tangled in the tree."

The warden gave a brief nod. "Very well. Run along now." He turned his back on them and continued speaking into the phone.

Lucy didn't move. Joe wondered if she was as annoyed by the dismissal as he was. He couldn't recall ever being told to 'run along'!

From the hallway, he heard the words 'disposal' and 'evacuation'. After a minute, the warden replaced the receiver. Seeing Lucy still standing there, he clapped his hands. "Shoo! Run along, I said! You've done what you had to, informing me. Now off you go.

We've enough to deal with without children under our feet!" In spite of his words, Joe sensed he was delighted to have something to do.

"How long will it take to defuse, do you think?" Lucy persisted.

"How long is a piece of string? I'm sure you know, it's a highly dangerous operation. Some bombs take days to defuse. The difficulty will depend on the precise position of the device. Even if the fuse is accessible, it's a lengthy and hazardous task to remove it. Now, go!"

He glanced over Lucy's shoulder at Joe. His eyes narrowed. "Don't I know -" he began. Fortunately, the telephone rang. He turned to answer it.

"Come on, Lucy! Let's go!" Joe didn't care if it seemed like he was obediently 'running along'. Postlethwaite had said he never forgot a face. Plainly, it hadn't been an empty boast.

Before they had reached the fence around the gardens of the bombed house, a van drew up beyond it and a man began unloading some wooden posts. Another arrived on a bicycle and set the posts on either side of the road, attaching a rope from one to the other to cordon off the street. Both men were wearing the same uniform and tin hats as Postlethwaite. The bicycle man looked to be a similar age, but his face was more rounded and pleasanter.

"Are you the children who found it?" he called to them, as the van drove away past them. "Hurry up now!" He beckoned to them urgently. "We wouldn't want you blown to bits, after you've managed to report the thing!" He moved the rope aside to let them pass and then held out his hand. "I'm Major Waters," he said. "Well done, young man, young lady!" He shook first Joe's hand and then Lucy's. "Now, I'm sure I can rely on you to stay on this side of the barrier while I go and empty the houses nearby."

"Of course!" Lucy was glowing. Joe, too, felt much happier to find Waters in charge rather than Postlethwaite. Mr. Waters had been a kindly man both times he'd met him. He wouldn't tell them off for nothing.

Joe looked back the way he and Lucy had come. A second cordon was being set up there, with another officer knocking on doors.

Major Waters went down the side street nearest the bombed house, and knocked on the first door. A woman with a baby on her hip appeared. Lucy and Joe were too far away to hear Major Waters' words, but the alarm on the woman's face was obvious. Within five minutes, she was hustling three young children out of the house, all wrapped in scarves and hats, while she carried the baby in a blanket. It was Lady Poston, Joe realised in surprise. She'd come down in the world since Cornwall, to be living in a little terraced house rather than a mansion!

Very soon, quite a crowd had gathered behind the cordons, mostly women and children, though there were a few elderly people as well. In the meantime, two men in uniform, both a good deal younger than Waters and Postlethwaite, had slipped past the rope and hurried up the street to the gap in the fence. Both carried toolboxes.

Having satisfied himself that there was nobody remaining in the houses nearest to his end of the street, Major Waters returned to the barrier. "Please do remain calm, ladies and gentleman," he said. "You've been asked to leave your homes merely as a precaution. In the event that the bomb detonates, your houses are unlikely to be affected.

"Some of you may have seen the bomb disposal squad go in already, and the WVS will be here shortly with their tea van. If you'd prefer to spend what may be a long wait indoors in the warm, may I suggest the church hall at Christ Church on Oxford Road. The good ladies there will look after you."

Joe looked around to see how people were responding to the situation. Someone had produced chairs for a particularly aged couple, who were sitting on the edge of them, muffled and querulous. Everyone else seemed to be resigned to the wait, or preoccupied with trying to decide what to do. Not one of them seemed annoyed by the interruption to their day, nor particularly anxious about the danger they'd unwittingly been in.

For a while, Joe and Lucy waited. Nothing further happened except that people joined the back of the crowd from time to time. Joe could hear them speculating.

"Don't know why nobody saw it before," someone said. "With the house gone, there was a clear view over the garden."

"I heard it fell last night," chimed in a woman.

"There was no raid last night," objected another.

"One rogue bomber maybe. Slipped past the air-raid detection, on his way back from somewhere else."

"Perhaps he got lost, looking for Manchester."

"Or decided he couldn't face going somewhere so miserable!" There was a chorus of laughter.

"Do you want to stay?" Joe asked Lucy.

"I don't think so. It could be hours, and I'm getting cold just standing here, aren't you? We could go to the park and come back later on." She looked at her watch. "It's nearly three. We need to be home by half five at the latest, but we could stop by and see if they've done it by then." She led the way back through the crowd and away along a side street.

There were other children already playing in the park. As Joe and Lucy crossed the grass, there was a wail as the smallest of a gaggle of children fell off a kind of swingboat. That must be the jerkers Lucy had mentioned, Joe thought, because beside it was a cone-shaped frame which had to be the witch's hat. Two boys were scrambling around the rim, taking it in turns to lean out so that it lurched under their weight.

It was strange to think that none of these kids

had any idea that there was a huge bomb just a few minutes walk from here. Stranger still was the fact that they might not be that interested if they did know.

"Imagine being the person who has to defuse it," Joe said to Lucy, as they sat down on the ordinary swings.

"I know!" Lucy pulled on the chains to set her swing moving. "If it goes off, he'll have no chance."

"He? Don't you mean they? There were two of them."

"One's the observer, though," she said, swinging higher. "The officer defusing the bomb calls to the observer to tell him what he's doing at each stage, and the observer writes it down. The observer has to be far enough away to have a good chance of surviving if it explodes."

"What's the point in him being there then?"

"Because that's how people have worked out how to do it! Now and then the Germans change the mechanism, so it's back to trial and error again. If the person defusing the bomb doesn't tell someone what he's doing, how would anyone ever know what *not* to do if it goes off?"

Joe nodded slowly. He'd never thought about how you might defuse a bomb. "How do you know so much about it?" he asked.

"Ma's brother did it during the Great War."

"Your Uncle Tom?"

"No, they had another brother, older than her,

younger than Tom."

Joe adjusted the speed he was swinging to match Lucy's rhythm. "Was he a conscientious objector then?"

She shook her head. "He joined up as a normal soldier, like Uncle Tom and all their friends. Defusing bombs was the job he was given. He was good at it, too." Joe could hear the 'but' coming. "But not good enough," she added.

"He was blown up?"

She nodded. "He was twenty years old. Ma told me once that if Uncle Tom hadn't been too old to serve in this war, he would have been a conchie because of what the last war did to their generation." She gave a short laugh. "Of course, he could have still ended up doing bomb disposal like his brother."

They swung for a while without speaking and then moved to the jerkers when the other children got off. Two of them were barefoot, Joe saw, just like Ellen had said. He shuddered. That was all very well in the summer, but not in November. Every time he stopped moving, he started to get cold, and he was much better dressed.

The street was still closed off when they got back to the bombsite a while later. A few people were standing beside the cordon but most had disappeared. A large green van was drawn up, with a hatch where the side window should have been. Two women stood behind this, making tea and sandwiches. One looked quite cheery while the other glowered. Joe was amused to recognise Mary Stanton, who'd worked for the Lucases in several worlds, and Miss Vincent, the grim-faced housekeeper from Tregaris.

"Is there any news?" Lucy asked Major Waters, who was still standing at the rope.

"None so far," he said. "I'm afraid it may well be past your bedtime before he gets it done, past all our bedtimes if it's a difficult one!"

"Are you the children that found the bomb?" asked a voice behind them.

Joe turned round. A man with a black beard was lounging against the tea van, a cigarette clamped in the corner of his mouth. A camera with a huge flash bulb was slung over his shoulder. He straightened up and came towards them.

"I'm Harry Close," he said. "I work for the Liverpool Echo."

Joe grinned. Another familiar face! Admittedly, he hadn't recognised the elderly couple here earlier, nor the butcher this morning, but he was prepared to bet they'd all been there in Lucy's other worlds, in the background somewhere.

"That's right!" Lucy beamed at the photographer.

"Very brave you were too, raising the alarm so calmly," Harry Close said. "Do you have a message you'd like to send to Corporal Carraway in there, while he works on the bomb?"

"Carraway?" Joe exclaimed. "That's Mr.

Carraway in there?"

"Corporal these days, not plain mister any more. You know him?" Close swung back towards Joe, who blushed scarlet.

"No, sorry, no," he gabbled. "I know a man called Carraway, but he couldn't be the same person. I don't think he lives in Liverpool."

"I know him," called Mary Stanton from the van. "Tom Carraway is my neighbour, and a very decent young man he is too. Certainly doing his bit for the country!"

The photographer pricked up his ears. "This is starting to sound like a story! Let's get some photos of you all." He began to fiddle with his camera. "This is exactly the sort of thing the people of Liverpool need to cheer them up!"

Joe sidled round behind Lucy. There was no way he could let Harry Close try and capture him on film. He knew that from the last world.

Suddenly, there was a buzz of interest around them. Two men were stepping out through the gap in the fencing. Joe didn't know the first, but the second was indeed Thomas Carraway from Lucy's Cornwall. They walked towards the rope where Joe and Lucy were standing.

"All safe," Carraway announced. "Private Dunning here will send a lorry round tomorrow to fetch the bomb, but the fuse has been safely removed." He held up a black cylinder with a long length of brown wire bundled at one end. The crowd cheered.

"Corporal Carraway!" Harry Close sprang forward. "If I might just take your photograph? One of the lovely WVS ladies is your neighbour, and these are the two children who found the bomb." He gestured to Lucy and Joe. "We'll get you in tomorrow's paper, 'Making Liverpool safe for everyone', or something like that. Come on, you two." Close stepped back into position as Mary Stanton climbed down from the van and made her way through the group to stand beside Tom Carraway.

"Come on!" Lucy tugged Joe's arm. "Don't be shy! What are you waiting for?"

"I can't!" he cried. "I can't be in the picture."

"Why not? If you're in the paper, that might help us find your family more quickly, instead of waiting for your mother to write back! Please, Sir," she called to the photographer, "my friend is searching for his lost relations. Could you include that in the article?"

"No!" Joe cried.

Too late. The flash bulb flared. "No problem at all!" Harry Close said with a broad smile. "One more time. Look this way please, young man!"

But Joe's gaze was locked on his feet in utter dismay.

8

"What's all this?" Lucy's father frowned and pushed his breakfast plate aside the next morning. The newspaper snapped as he folded it over. "Why are you in that picture, Lucy?" He jabbed the page with his finger. "What are you doing in the paper at all?"

Joe glanced across. His heart plummeted. A split second was enough to confirm what he'd known from the moment the photographer had started lining up the shot: he wasn't beside Lucy in the photograph. Just like last time, he hadn't appeared on the film.

But it wasn't Joe's absence from the picture that had caught William's attention. Lucy's father began to read aloud. "*The 1000kg parachute bomb was found by Lucy Lucas, aged twelve, of Bootle, while she and her friend were playing in the gardens of a house which received a direct hit in September*." He glared at his daughter. "What do you have to say for yourself?"

Lucy stared at her plate. She didn't answer.

"I think you'll agree, it's you the article is talking

about. There aren't two Lucy Lucases aged twelve in Bootle. And even if there were, they wouldn't both look like you." He read on in silence.

Joe looked across at Lucy. She'd gone white.

The seconds stretched out. At last, William had finished the article. There was another long pause. Then, "Haven't you listened to anything we've told you?"

Still Lucy said nothing.

"Or do you think you're somehow special? Little Lucy can dance through the ruins with never so much as a scratch! Tell me you *do* know why you shouldn't go into bombsites!"

Lucy nodded.

"Why is that?"

"Because it's dangerous," she mumbled.

"Exactly. Because it's dangerous," William repeated. "We've talked about what those dangers are: falling bricks and timbers, gas, broken glass. Maybe we didn't include unexploded bombs on the list, but I'd have thought the danger of getting close to one of those was obvious!" He tossed the newspaper across the table towards his wife. "Did you know about this?"

Ellen picked it up. "Oh, Lucy," she said, her voice heavy with disappointment. "You said you went to fetch the warden, but that was only half the truth, wasn't it? Less than half of it, in fact. Why didn't you tell me you'd found the bomb?"

"I knew you'd be cross." Lucy's words were

scarcely more than a murmur.

"Quite right! It's just as your father says: you shouldn't have been playing there at all! Think what could have happened!"

Lucy hung her head. "I'm sorry. The gardens are so lovely. We didn't go near the ruins of the house," she added, in an outright lie.

"And what was Joe doing while you were doing all this? He's not in the photograph, I see. I assume he was sensibly keeping his distance."

Joe cringed.

The line of Lucy's jaw hardened. "I don't know why he's not in the picture!" she said, abruptly furious. "He was standing right next to me. We were together the whole time." Joe waited for her to remember his reluctance to be photographed. If she asked him about that now, in front of her parents, he didn't know what he'd say.

William cut in, however. "That's even worse, Lucy! He's a visitor here, our guest. You know very well that he was evacuated before the bombs started falling. If he doesn't know the dangers, it's hardly any wonder! It was up to you to look after him. We trusted you." Lucy's father wasn't shouting any more, but somehow that was worse. "I see you asked the journalist to mention Joe's family, so you must have been thinking fairly clearly! Imagine if that bomb had gone off while you were beside it! This would have been Joe's death notice!" He snatched up the paper

101

again. "Enough people are being killed every day because of the war without a naughty girl adding to them!"

Lucy squirmed in her chair. Opposite her, Joe looked down at his plate. This situation was as much his fault as hers. True, he might not have been able to stop her going into the bombsite, but it hadn't even occurred to him to try. He'd wanted to go in there every bit as much as she did. The only difference was that he wouldn't have spoken to Harry Close about it. If it had been up to him, Lucy's parents wouldn't have found out what had happened. That would have saved them from getting told off, but he and Lucy would still have been in the wrong.

There was the problem of the photograph as well. That, at least, could have been avoided. As he helped Lucy clear the table, he dreaded the moment they would be alone together. She was bound to demand an explanation for why he wasn't in the picture.

While he helped her wash and dry the breakfast things, however, Ellen and William were arguing so loudly in the next room that neither he nor Lucy spoke. William was adamant that Lucy should be kept at home for a week at least, even though that would mean missing lessons. Ellen pointed out that she couldn't give up everything she had to do just to be Lucy's jailer. If they were going to trust her not to go out while they were out themselves, she said, they might as well trust her not to do something so stupid ever again.

At last, the front door banged shut. Lucy gave a whistle of relief, which she disguised hastily as a cough at the sight of her mother's stony face.

"I'm sure you heard all that," Ellen said, coming into the kitchen. "I expect half the street did, too. At least I managed to persuade your father not to insist on keeping you at home."

Lucy flung her arms around her mother. "Thank you!"

"But –" Ellen disentangled herself coldly from Lucy's embrace. "This can't go unpunished. First of all, I want you to promise me absolutely that you will never go into any bombsite ever again, for any reason."

"I promise," Lucy said meekly.

"If you break that promise, I will not defend you from whatever …" she paused and looked Lucy in the eye, "from *whatever* punishment your father thinks fit, even if he decides to take his belt to you!"

Lucy blanched. "I promise, I really do!"

"Second, I expect you to make amends for letting us down like this. For the next month, you'll do whatever chores I decide, with no complaints and no shirking. I can tell you now, they'll be the things I most hate doing. You can start this minute by fetching the chamber pots from under the beds and emptying and scouring them out, and if I hear the slightest grumble –" She left the sentence unfinished.

Lucy went out of the room at once, leaving Joe twisting the damp tea towel between his hands.

"I'm sorry about this," Ellen said. "I'm afraid the atmosphere here isn't going to be very nice for the next little while. I daresay you'll be glad to move on. Let's hope your uncle and aunt see the article and contact the newspaper. It's a pity you weren't in the picture, though I suppose if you've never met, that's neither here nor there."

Joe didn't know how to answer. Instead, he said, "I'm very sorry, Mrs Lucas. It was my fault as much as Lucy's. She did say we weren't supposed to go in there, but I wanted to." Before she could reply, he went on, "I'd like to make myself useful for as long as I'm staying. I expect my uncle will get in touch soon, but until then, what can I do to be helpful?"

Ellen smiled wearily, her fury spent. "You could fetch the coal in again." Her eyes fell on a cloth-wrapped parcel on the kitchen table. "I'll get you to run down to the docks in a bit, too. That's William's lunch I made him. He was in such a state, he's forgotten to take it!" She shook her head. "It would be better if you go rather than Lucy. If he sees her down there today, he might just blow his top!"

Joe nodded.

Two hours later, he was making his way through the back streets of Bootle towards the River Mersey. In one hand he had William's food, in the other a scrap of paper with a map Ellen had scribbled for him. It was little more than a few lines and some road names with the occasional arrow. He wished Lucy was with him to help him work out where to go, but it was impossible not to see the sense in her keeping out of William's way for a while.

Besides, as she'd pointed out, Joe would be much less conspicuous down at the docks without her, since there would be very few women and no girls there. She'd found him an old cap and jacket of Peter's and made him take off his tie and leave his coat at home in spite of the cold, so that he looked less like a schoolboy. If he could pass himself off as an apprentice docker, she said, this could be the perfect chance to try and find out more about what was going on with Jackson and Metcalfe. All he had to do was find out where they worked, she added cheerfully, as though it was the easiest thing in the world. For his own part, Joe hoped he would run into Amos instead. The sailor wasn't due to leave Liverpool until tomorrow. Perhaps he'd managed to gather more information about what the others were up to.

When he finally found his way through the last of the terraces to the docks, however, Joe realised what an absurdly foolish hope this had been. It hadn't occurred to him how big the place might be! The river was broad and the waterfront stretched away out of sight in both directions, a scarred edge to a monstrous landscape of concrete and steel.

Joe put back his shoulders and tried not to feel dwarfed by the immense hulls of ships that loomed above him. Crates were stacked up, awaiting the cranes which towered beside the ships, swivelling around like giant, angular birds. It smelled of seawater here, but also of coal and fumes. The clanking he'd heard distantly on the first evening was much louder too, metal hammering against metal, and there was the grinding of chains, and now and then a squeal from something needing oil.

It was a far cry from the port he'd seen in Bristol, he thought. There, the quayside had been more crowded with people, and the river more full of ships. But it had been a smaller river and smaller ships. Everything had been on a much more human scale. Here, he felt like an insect in danger of being squashed.

He looked around for some sign of where to go, and then down at Ellen's instructions again. She'd explained how to find William, but if he was going to make use of being here, he should put off delivering the lunch parcel for as long as possible, to have a ready excuse for anyone who asked what he was doing.

There were a few men around, though not as many as Joe had imagined, and some boys not much older than himself. All of them seemed busy. Joe knew he'd have to look busy too, if he was to avoid drawing attention to himself. But how? What could he do?

Where should he go? Even the familiar sight of Jackson or Metcalfe would at least tell him he was in the right place, though quite what that would achieve, he didn't know.

He set off towards a low building, for somewhere to go rather than for any better reason. Then he saw something, or rather someone, he hadn't expected. A man in a dark overcoat and hat came out of the building, carrying a briefcase. He paused for a moment and checked his watch, then looked quickly around and marched off.

Joe quickened his pace to follow. The man was a short distance ahead of him, not hurrying, yet moving with a briskness that suggested official business. Joe might not have recognised him from so far away, with his features shadowed by his hat. But there had already been so many familiar people in this world, he must have started unconsciously looking for faces he knew. This was certainly one of them: Morley, the steward from Old Wardour Castle, who had turned up in Bristol as the butler. Joe winced as he recalled their last encounter. It was just as well that cuts and bruises healed as he passed back into his own time, or he'd have been black and blue for weeks.

For a few minutes, he followed Morley through the docklands. The man kept mostly to a cobbled roadway that ran between cranes and crates. Joe took care not to let the gap between them narrow. He had no desire to explain to Morley what he was doing, even though Morley wasn't carrying a stick this time. Of course, it might be a wild goose chase anyway. Morley might have been doing something quite innocent, and be on his way home now for lunch.

Yet Joe couldn't shake the feeling that it was significant that he'd turned up here of all places. For one thing, it was clear from his clothes that he didn't work here – he was much too smartly dressed. If anything, the coat and briefcase made Joe think of a bank manager or government official, which made Morley seem especially out of place.

It was more than that, though. Morley was unlikely to be here by chance: if the cast of characters was gathering together from all his past times with Lucy, the most important of them must have a role to play in this final world. Joe swallowed and mentally deleted the word 'final'. He didn't know for sure this was the last time. Perhaps when he got to the end here, the clock would turn over like an egg timer, and he would be plunged back in at the start again. How much better he would manage second time round! For a few moments, he indulged in happy imaginings of himself as a Roman or Viking again. He would know so much more next time, and he wouldn't end up tripping over silly details or asking stupid questions.

Perhaps it was because he wasn't concentrating on the present that what happened next took him by surprise. Morley had disappeared from view as the track bent round behind some crates. Joe wasn't worried. His target had moved out of sight several times in the last few minutes, but he'd picked up the trail easily enough a few paces further on. He rounded the bend.

This time, the roadway stretched out, empty. Morley had vanished.

Joe halted. Where had he gone? Had he realised he was being followed, and ducked out of the way in order to lose Joe? Joe looked all around, but could see no sign of him. That didn't make sense anyway – there was no reason for a grown man to fear an unarmed thirteen year old. He probably wouldn't suspect Joe of anything except maybe hoping to pick his pocket. All he had to do was turn and confront him, and Joe would be left floundering to explain himself.

He walked on, his footsteps less certain now. He felt unpleasantly exposed; anyone who saw him would know he had no business here! Of course, he reminded himself, Morley wouldn't recognise him even if he'd noticed him.

At the side of the road ahead was a delivery van. Joe had seen a few other vans drawn up, being loaded or unloaded. He was about to walk past when the name on the side caught his eye. Peekes. That was the greengrocer he'd been to with Lucy, where Tobias worked. This couldn't possibly be a coincidence! But surely even if Peekes knew Tobias was selling food on the black market, even if he was in on it, he wouldn't be so brazen as to drive the shop van down here to collect the goods in broad daylight!

Joe glanced in as he drew level with the cab of the van. Without meaning to, he stopped dead.

Sitting in the driver's seat just the other side of the glass was Tobias. His face was turned away, but there was no mistaking the wavy hair. He wasn't alone either. Through the window, Joe could hear the murmur of voices. Two more men were squeezed into the cab beyond Tobias. The one on the far side was Morley.

Joe peered over Tobias' shoulder trying to see who was sitting in the middle. Too late, he realised he'd been seen. Tobias' head whipped round. He looked Joe full in the face. Joe's stomach dropped. There was no doubt Tobias recognised him from the previous day. He should never have asked where the oranges had come from.

The latch of the van door clicked, but before Tobias could shove it open, Joe spun round and sprinted back the way he'd come. Running footsteps and shouting told him he was being followed. Joe zigzagged off the track between the heaps of crates and sacks.

On he ran, changing direction at random, straining his ears to know if Tobias had given up. He couldn't be sure and he didn't dare stop for long enough to check. Besides, the surprised faces of the men he passed would act as markers for Tobias, pointing him the right way.

Suddenly, Joe was trapped. In front of him was the water, and half a dozen men unloading a ship; behind him, he could hear pounding feet; the ship's cargo blocked his way to the right; and some railway goods carriages cut off the left. He looked desperately around. If the dockers saw him, they would probably stop him. He could try and hide, but he had only a few seconds at most.

"Psst! Here!"

Joe whirled round. The sliding side of one of the railway carriages was partly open. It was dark inside. Joe couldn't see who was there, but he had no choice. Any moment now, Tobias would reach him, or the dockers would spot him. He darted towards the carriage and grabbed the hand that reached out to haul him up.

9

He tumbled into the darkness, banging his elbow and his ankle and dropping William's lunch packet on the floor of the wagon. "Ow!" He rubbed his arm and tried to get his breath back.

"Sssh!"

Joe still couldn't see his rescuer, but he knew who it was. "Amos?" he whispered.

"Yes, it's me. Keep quiet."

As Joe's eyes adjusted, he saw Amos move noiselessly away from the open side of the goods wagon to look out through a grating further along.

"Thank you for saving me!" Joe murmured.

Amos flapped his hand. "I might not have yet. Stay out of sight."

Joe drew his knees up and huddled in the corner, away from the door. The wagon was empty. There was nothing to hide behind if his pursuer decided to look in here.

"Was it Jackson chasing you?" Amos muttered.

Joe frowned. "I thought it was Tobias," he said. "He was the one with Jackson and Metcalfe on Tuesday evening. I suppose it could have been both of them."

"Jackson's just come running, that's all. He looks flustered."

"Is Tobias with him?"

"No. What are you doing down here anyway?"

"I brought William Lucas' lunch. He forgot to take it this morning."

Amos turned towards Joe. His grin was white in the gloom. "Of course! That explains everything. Jackson is chasing you because he likes corned beef sandwiches so much!"

Joe chuckled. "I just thought while I was down here, I'd see if I could find out anything about what you said when we met."

Amos shook his head. "That's for the authorities to deal with, not a boy like you!"

"You said they wouldn't listen to you!"

"You think they'll listen to you?"

"No," Joe admitted. "But that doesn't mean we shouldn't try. There's someone else as well. I don't know how he's connected, but I've just followed him. His name's Morley."

"How do you know? What makes you think he

has anything to do with it?"

"Because he's —" Joe hesitated. "I can't explain how I know," he said lamely. "But I know I'm right. Anyway, I'm not the only one who's somewhere they shouldn't be. What's a sailor doing hiding in a railway carriage?"

Amos gestured to another grating above Joe's head. "Watching Metcalfe. Stanford's over there too. He's the one with the list." Joe got to his feet and peeped out. Amos tiptoed along the wagon towards him, keeping in the shadows as he passed the open door. "That's Metcalfe, waiting for the cargo."

A collection of sacks had been bundled into a net which was being lowered slowly on a cable from one of the huge cranes. As it came within reach, Metcalfe and another man caught hold of the net with large hooks, and guided it down onto the open back of a lorry. Metcalfe unclipped the cable, and he and three other men unloaded the sacks. Stanford stood idly by, his hat tipped back on his head. As the empty cargo net was clipped back on and lifted away, he marked something on his notepad.

"What's in the sacks?" Joe asked.

"I don't know," Amos replied. "Food of some sort. Flour maybe, or sugar."

"If it is, and Metcalfe's waiting for his chance to steal some, then why is Peekes' van parked so far from

114

the ship? How is Metcalfe going to get the stuff over there without getting caught?"

"He can use a sack truck, just like those men there." Amos nodded to two flat-capped dockers stacking crates onto a frame with a pair of handles and two iron wheels. "If you're collecting goods that aren't yours to take, you wouldn't want to be too close, would you? Better that nobody makes the link between your transport and the ship. Metcalfe doesn't need to worry about getting caught, though. It's Stanford who should notice him, but in a moment, he'll pretend to be distracted. After that, Metcalfe's clear to go. Of course, as soon as he's wheeled his prize round the corner, no-one who sees him will know what's in the boxes or sacks, nor where it should be going." He raised his eyebrows. "You said Peekes' van. Who is Peekes?"

Joe told him about the greengrocer, and about the oranges the day before.

"I still don't think that's everything that's going on, though," he said. Jackson was visible through this grating now. He seemed to have given up looking for Joe and was approaching the dockers. "It might be a sideline," Joe went on thoughtfully, "to make a bit of money. But the other man, Morley, wasn't dressed like any of these, not even Stanford. He looked much more important."

Amos threw Joe a look. "You think he's got

something to do with the aircraft parts?"

Joe frowned. "That might be it. I suppose there would have to be somebody in charge of a sabotage operation, and it wouldn't necessarily be one of the engineers." A thought came to him. "What if he's a spy? What if he's collecting information for the Germans?"

"What sort of information?"

"You said yourself that the ships still have to cross the Atlantic, even though the U-Boats are out there waiting for them. Wouldn't it be useful for the Germans to know which ships are leaving when, and what routes they plan to take? That would make it much easier for the wolfpacks to find them."

In the gloom, Joe saw Amos' eyes widen. "I hope to God you're wrong," he said. "It's dangerous enough as it is, without people here helping the other side." He looked away.

Joe was silent. Amos' words hung in the air. The other side. The wrong side. Jackson had said Tobias should avoid being called up for the wrong side, yet he was about to be called up to fight for the British. There was only one way that remark could make sense.

"Forget it," he said, trying to sound casual. "It's probably nothing to do with that." He nodded to the grating. "What are we going to do about what's happening out there, though?"

Amos considered. "I don't know if we can do anything. If only we had a camera, we might be able to get a photograph of them, but it would still be hard to prove they were stealing the goods, not just moving them around."

"I met a photographer yesterday," Joe said. "He might be interested in helping us get proof if he could write an article about it." As soon as the words were out, he regretted the suggestion. Harry Coles would be certain to remember him as the boy who hadn't appeared in the picture. That could get him into all kinds of trouble.

Fortunately, Amos shook his head. "Petty theft won't interest the papers when there's so much else going on. And if it's sabotage or passing information to the Germans, it's too important to expose like that. The culprits would have to be caught red-handed by the authorities, so they can be locked up and the keys thrown away!"

Amos spoke with barely contained passion. Of course, if he believed Joe was right about Morley being a spy, it was hardly any wonder. Joe wished he hadn't said it. It was terrible even to suspect such a thing if you couldn't do anything to stop it.

Amos gave himself a shake. "I think you've done enough sneaking around for one day, young man. You'd better get that lunch parcel over to William

Lucas before he starts getting hungry."

"Did you speak to him about the thefts?" Joe asked.

"I did." Amos shrugged. "I don't think he's had any more luck than I have. If you want to get your voice heard in this world, you need to be posh and white, and a man. I'm only one of those things, and so are you. Even William Lucas is only two, which isn't enough."

Morley was probably all three, Joe thought, as he climbed quietly down from the wagon. People would listen to him. Joe gave a brief wave to Amos and darted away between the railway carriages, back round to where he'd come from earlier on. If Morley was on the wrong side of this war, there was very little that he, Amos, or William would be able to do about it.

Joe told Lucy all about the morning's events as they walked across Liverpool after lunch, to the house where her lessons were taking place today. He described Morley without mentioning his name, since he couldn't say how he knew it. He couldn't tell her either why he was so very sure that Morley was involved in Tobias and Jackson's scheme. Nonetheless, she seemed to accept that Morley sitting in the van with Tobias was enough. They were still mid-conversation when Lucy had to leave Joe on the doorstep to go inside for her classes.

Joe wandered aimlessly for the next two hours while he waited for her to finish. This seemed to be one of the wealthier districts of the city, and there was no bomb damage at all. There were a few cars on the street, old-fashioned vehicles like he'd seen in films, and the lamp posts were old-fashioned too. Other than that, he could have been in his own world.

He'd scarcely thought about the present since he arrived, he realised. Sooner or later though, he would be thrown back into it. He had to make sure Lucy at least had his St. Christopher before that happened, even if he didn't tell her what to do with it. His stomach clenched again at the prospect of confessing the truth to her. He was more tempted than ever simply to avoid it.

What he couldn't avoid was having to explain the photo in the newspaper: as soon as Lucy emerged from the house, she asked, "Why weren't you in the picture we had taken yesterday?"

Joe was caught completely by surprise. He'd presumed they would continue their conversation about Morley and the port. After all, she hadn't brought up the photograph this morning or on the way here, although there had been several opportunities.

For a moment, he was speechless. Then he said, "I thought you'd forgotten about it."

She stared at him. "Forgotten? How could I forget? It's hardly the sort of thing that happens every day!"

"It *has* happened before, actually," Joe mumbled.

"What?" This time Lucy stopped walking. "What did you just say?"

"It's happened before. That's why I didn't want to be in the photo."

Her mouth dropped open. "Why? How?"

Joe turned over possible answers in his mind. "There's something about me that stops me showing up on film," he said vaguely. He wondered whether to add that it was a condition, like a kind of health problem. She'd never believe that though, so there was nothing to be gained from the lie.

"Something about you? Like what? You're not a ghost, are you?" Lucy seized his fingers and pinched them hard between her own.

"Ouch! What did you do that for?"

"Just checking! I didn't think you were. You're as solid as I am, and everyone else can see you too. So if we're not imagining you, what in the world is it?"

Joe waggled the colour back into his fingers. "Why didn't you ask me when we were walking over here?" he said, hoping to distract her.

"I wanted to hear about this morning. Besides, I

was trying to think if there was any possible explanation. I couldn't think of anything, so tell me!"

Joe sighed. If this *was* the last time he would be in Lucy's world, at least it was the last time he would have to go through this. "I'm a time-traveller," he said shortly. "I live in the twenty-first century, almost eighty years from now. I use this to travel back into the past." He fished for the chain of his St. Christopher behind his collar and pulled it out. Unfastening the catch, he held it out to Lucy.

She peered at the pendant on his palm but didn't touch it.

"Take it," Joe said. "You need to have it."

"Why?" She backed away. "I don't want to go back in time! I want to go forward, and find out who's going to win the war."

"Britain will," Joe said. He dropped the St. Christopher into his coat pocket. It was clear she wouldn't accept it at the moment. He'd have to try again later. "America will join us and we'll defeat Germany in the end, though it's going to take another five years. The war won't end until 1945."

She gazed at him. "You really mean that, don't you? You think that's what will happen."

"I don't 'think'. I know," he said, with a touch of irritation. "It's a historical fact. We learn about the Second World War at school: 1939 to 1945."

For a few moments, she didn't speak. Then she said, "You're mad!"

Joe shook his head. "I know why you think that. If I were you, I'd think the same. But it really is true. If I could get home and look on the internet, I could probably find out when Liverpool's worst air raids will be, maybe even which streets are going to be hit. Of course, it'd be no good unless I could get back here in time to tell you."

A spark of curiosity appeared in Lucy's eyes. "What's the internet?" she asked. Before he could answer, she said, "I can't believe I just asked that! For a second, you had me! You should be a fortune-teller. I bet you could make all sorts up, and people would fall for it."

Joe shrugged. "It doesn't matter if you don't believe me now," he said. "At some point in the next day or two, I'll vanish into thin air, hopefully in front of you, and then you'll see I'm telling the truth." He walked on. At least part of his anxiety had lifted from his shoulders. If she wouldn't listen, that was her problem. He'd been honest with her, even if he hadn't told her the bit about her other worlds.

She caught him up. "Alright then, just supposing you're not making this up, what's it like in the time you come from, whenever that is?"

"It's the year 2016." He paused, trying to think

where to start describing his world to her. "In my time, quite a bit looks the same as here, but there are some things that have changed. Take a street like this," he gestured around. "There would be a lot of parked cars, because every house would have at least one car, sometimes two. There's a lot more traffic too, especially at this time of day, with people picking up their children from school, or driving home from work, and there are lots more lorries and trucks than you have here. So in Liverpool in my time, it's much noisier. There are quite a lot of fumes, too, though not the coal smell you've got."

"Why not?" Lucy's curiosity had got the better of her.

"We have central heating to warm our houses, radiators in all the rooms, not open fires. Some people cook on gas like you, although with much bigger stoves, but some use electric. We have a lot of things that use electricity: dishwashers and microwaves, washing machines, laptops, tablets, mobile phones, lots of lights everywhere, music."

"It sounds amazing! Are *all* the rooms in the house warm?"

"If you want, yes."

"But no coal to bring in, or fires to lay or clean out? Lights everywhere?" She sounded wistful. "We used to have lovely bright lights in the evenings, especially just before Christmas. Now there's the black-out, and we're supposed to save electricity for the war effort, too."

Joe thought for a moment. "We should be doing more of that at home where I come from. People in my world are just starting to realise how much energy we're using, and how everyone throws away more stuff than they should, packaging and plastic bottles, and other stuff. It's a lot more comfortable to live there than here, and everything's much easier, but it's not all better."

They walked on in silence for a while. Then Lucy said, "I'd love to come back with you, when you do go home."

Joe looked at her. "You believe me, then?"

"I suppose so. I mean, it's crazy to think someone could actually travel through time. That part is really hard to believe. But the way you talk about it, either you've really been there or you've got an incredible imagination."

Joe laughed. "Thanks! I can tell you, if I was going to imagine a place to live, I'd make it perfect – no rubbish, no climate change, no wars."

"There are wars there, too?"

"Not like this one you're in, not actually happening in Britain. But people are still fighting in different countries, and we still have refugees like –"

He broke off. The most hideous sound was suddenly blaring out all around them. It swooped up in pitch, a siren of some kind. He grabbed Lucy's arm. "What the hell is that?" It seemed to be coming from everywhere.

Lucy's face had drained of colour. She looked at her watch and then up at the sky. "It's early tonight!" Joe could hear her trying to contain her panic. "It might be a false alarm. Still, we'd better get a move on! Let's hope we have time to get home!"

She started to run. "Come on, Joe! Hurry up! It's an air raid!"

10

Together they ran through the streets as fast as they dared. It was nearly half past five and the sky overhead was almost completely dark. Without street lamps to light their way, pillar boxes, trees and even the lamp posts themselves loomed out of the darkness with alarming suddenness. Joe's boots slipped on lumps and bumps in the pavement. Lucy's satchel was bouncing heavily against her.

"How long have we got?" he yelled over the siren.

"Not sure. Ten minutes, maybe."

"Ten minutes? What, until they start dropping bombs on us?"

"Could be."

"That's not much warning!"

"They don't sound the alarm until they're sure the bombers are heading for Liverpool rather than Manchester," Lucy panted. "Usually it takes the planes a bit longer than that to get here, but sometimes there are one or two ahead of the rest."

They ran on. Joe was glad he was fit. It would have been embarrassing if he'd struggled to keep up with Lucy. "How far are we from your house?"

"Fifteen or twenty minutes if we were walking. We should just make it. Mind the kerb there!"

Lucy's warning came too late. Joe stumbled. His ankle turned over. He cursed.

She halted. "Are you alright?" Tension made her voice tight. "You have to run on if you can."

Joe flexed his foot. It was probably okay. It would have to be. He set off again, more cautiously now. "Wouldn't we be better off going into one of these shelters?" he called, as they passed another of the brick buildings.

"We'll have to, if the planes get to us before we get home. I really don't want to, though. It means spending the whole night among strangers, with no supper, no blankets, nothing to do. Ma would be worried sick, too. She always says we should stay together. That's the most important thing, wherever we are. At least then if one of us goes, we all go."

She sped up a little.

Joe made himself run faster. That was an awful thing to have to decide, whether it was better to save part of the family or all die together.

They didn't speak now. Joe was watching where he placed his feet, not looking more than half a dozen steps ahead at any time. All the same, he was aware that there were more people around than there had been before. Figures flitted past, hurrying to shelters or trying to get home just like they were.

As they crossed a larger road, he had a fleeting view of the sky over the city, criss-crossed by searchlights. Their beams swung to and fro, scanning the air for the oncoming planes. An air raid warden shouted. In the distance, there was a low humming sound.

"Quick! They're nearly here!" Lucy's voice was shrill. "We're so close! We have to make it!" She dashed, helter skelter, out into the middle of the road. Joe followed. There were no cars, only a couple of bicycles, and some other people who'd abandoned the pavement.

At last, he recognised Lucy's street. They flung themselves through her front door and kicked it shut. Joe felt a surge of relief that they'd got here. Somehow, it felt so much safer to be indoors rather than outside in the road. He knew that was absurd, given what a bomb would do if it fell on the house.

The hallway was in total darkness except for a wavy line of light along the floor in front of the kitchen door. The siren had stopped, but Joe's ears were still ringing.

"Is that you?" Lucy's mother cried out from somewhere ahead of them. "Thank God! Hurry up! Peter and I are under here already. I think we've got everything."

A flickering light lit up the hall. Ellen had drawn back a curtain beneath the stairs and was holding up a candle on a saucer. "In you come, quick now." She held the curtain aside. Joe wondered whether this was the entrance to a cellar, but beyond the curtain was just the triangular space under the staircase. It was even smaller than it might have been because of what looked like lengths of telegraph poles nailed along one wall and up the sloping ceiling.

Peter was already sitting on a wedge of blanket on the floor with his legs crossed and his arms clasped round them. He looked as if he'd had to be folded up just to get in. Joe shed his coat on the hall floor and squeezed past an upturned crate that was serving as a makeshift table. He sat down beside Peter as Lucy threw down her satchel and climbed in next to her mother.

Ellen drew the curtain across again and put the candle on the crate. "I'm so glad you're here!" She pulled Lucy close and kissed the top of her head. "I was afraid you wouldn't get back in time. They've never come before about seven, have they, except for the odd daylight raids, I suppose."

"They wanted to make sure we didn't get our tea!" Peter said. "Keep the enemy hungry and they'll give up fighting!"

Ellen grinned. "I'll go out once the first wave has gone past, and see what I can salvage." She looked at Joe. "This is your first air raid, I suppose?"

Joe nodded, glad that he didn't have to pretend otherwise.

"When the sirens go, we have to douse any fires that are lit and turn off the gas, which means no lights or cooker. I was in the middle of getting tea, but whether any of it will be edible I don't know! It's just as well everyone else is at work," she added. "What would we have done if this had happened on Tuesday?"

"It would have been worse than sardines!" Lucy laughed. "We'd never have got Amos Harper under here with us, as well as Uncle Tom and Aunt Jane!"

The hum had swelled to a drone. It sounded like a swarm of bees on the other side of the curtain now. Joe looked at the piece of material, puzzled. What use was that if a bomb fell? Maybe it was just to cover this space during the day. With the reinforced wall and ceiling, it did look a bit like a building site under here.

He heard a far off crump, and then another, a little closer.

"Let's have the playing cards then, Peter," Ellen said brightly.

Peter drew a box from his pocket and tipped the pack into his hand. "We'll play rummy, shall we?"

Another explosion. A fourth, a fifth. In between, ear-splitting whistles, like demented fireworks. They weren't fireworks, though. Fireworks weren't intended to kill people.

Joe watched Peter shuffle the cards and deal them out on the crate. How could anyone concentrate on a game with all that going on out there?

The engines of the planes were loud now. They must be right above them. Joe found he was holding his breath. To distract himself, he tried to think through the dangers he'd faced in Lucy's worlds. This must be the biggest, the most indiscriminate, much worse than Tobias with his knives or gun.

Except that wasn't right – the Great Fire of London had been wholly indiscriminate, just as dangerous, maybe even worse. That had turned out alright in the end, for Lucy's family at least. Maybe this would be fine too.

The explosions were coming one after another now, some quite distant, others terrifyingly near. All the time, the whistling went on, drowned out only by the roar as a building or road was torn apart. Joe picked up his cards and looked at Lucy and Ellen.

Their faces were taut with waiting. There was no logic in assuming they were all going to be fine. There was no logic in any of it. Whether or not they survived depended on the precise second at which a man up in the sky flicked a switch. A moment's difference could wipe them all out.

But surely that couldn't happen, Joe thought. Any bomb that got Lucy would get him too. He couldn't be flung back into his own time dead! He closed his eyes. It was better not to think about it.

He didn't know how long the bombardment went on. It might only have been minutes. It felt like hours. At last, the explosions seemed to be getting further away, as though the bombers had chosen a new target.

Then came a deafening blast. Lucy shrank down in her corner, her eyes screwed shut. The whole house shook. Joe heard the smash of falling china in the parlour. He threw his arms over his head and waited for upstairs to crash down on them.

There was only a trickle of dust.

"Was that this street, do you think?" Lucy asked after almost a minute.

"Olivia Street, I reckon," Peter answered, "poor buggers."

"Peter! Language!" Ellen cried. Then she burst out laughing. "I can't believe I just said that!" she exclaimed. "Here we are, a few hundred feet from destruction, and I'm telling you off for swearing! I'm sure the Lord would forgive you even if that was the very last thing you said!"

Peter grinned. "Thank Him, it hasn't been!"

Lucy began to giggle. Joe started to laugh too, though he hardly knew why. More than anything, it felt good just to be alive!

"I wonder how your father's getting on," Ellen said to Peter and Lucy.

"What's he doing?" Joe asked.

"He's a fire warden. Every one of those whistles was an incendiary bomb. They have to be dealt with quickly, or they set light to everything around them. The fire wardens and firemen are going to be busy tonight."

"I wish I was on duty!" Peter said.

"I'm glad you're not," Ellen retorted. "I'd hate you to be out there on a night like this."

"But quiet nights are so boring!"

"What do you actually do?" Joe asked.

Peter drew himself up in the tiny space. "I cycle around the city, taking messages to and from the control centre so that fire crews know where they're most needed."

"Really?" Joe couldn't help but be impressed. That was real war work, not just playing at it.

"Racing between the bullets on your trusty

bike!" Lucy giggled again. "Except you haven't been on duty during a big raid, have you?"

"I have too, back in October! It's the luck of the draw! If this had happened on Tuesday, you might have been trying to squeeze that sailor in here, but I'd have been out in the streets."

Lucy opened her mouth to reply, but Ellen put up her hand. "Don't tease," she said. "Do you have a little sister, Joe?"

"No."

"Lucky you!" Peter growled.

Ellen had relaxed enough to smile. "Their whole mission in life is to stop their older brothers getting too big for their boots! Peter's right – if this had been Tuesday, he would have been out in it. Now, I'm going to go and investigate the tea while it's quiet."

"What time is it?" Lucy asked.

Her mother looked at her watch and groaned. "Only just past seven! I thought it was much later than that. If the food didn't finish cooking after I turned the gas off, we'll have bread and butter. It's better than nothing."

"Shall I come and help?" Lucy volunteered.

"No, better that you stay safe under here." She lit a second candle from the first and melted some wax to stick it on a plate.

"Hasn't it finished, then?" Joe was taken aback.

"That was just the first wave," Peter said, clearly keen to reassert his authority. "If that was the end of it, they'd be sounding the all clear. It'll probably go on another six or eight hours at least."

"So what do we do now?"

"Nip out to the loo if you think you need to. And we'll eat whatever supper Ma can rescue. Then we play cards and wait."

"How long until the next wave?"

Peter shrugged. "Could be a couple of hours. Might only be a few minutes. That's why we stay under here unless we're desperate for a pee."

Joe hadn't thought he was, but now that Peter had mentioned it twice, he felt as though he couldn't wait another moment.

"You know, I think I will go out, while I can." He crawled across Peter and past the curtain, following Ellen into the kitchen. It was good to be able to stand up straight again and stretch his legs. It might not be much after seven o'clock, but that still meant they'd been under there for well over an hour, and he'd been as tense as a spring for most of that time.

The kitchen was dim, lit only by Ellen's candle. She gave him a small torch to light his way out to the privy, but when he stepped outside, he found he didn't need it. The sky was orange from the fires, particularly in one direction. Maybe that was the docks. They must be a major target for the enemy.

Joe turned on the spot, gazing up. It had been quite cloudy as he'd run home with Lucy, but not like this. Now, a thick grey blanket lay over Liverpool, suffocating the city beneath its acrid weight. He stood on tiptoe and craned his neck to see which house had just been hit. There seemed to be a gap in the next terrace, behind Lucy's house, which hadn't been there before. Had the family been inside, huddled under the stairs like them? Would you even know you'd been hit? Probably not.

In the close darkness of the privy, he mused over whether Ellen was right to keep everyone at home. Staying together made sense, though since William didn't seem to be at home much, that would mean he'd lose his whole family if the house was hit. On the other hand, the randomness of the bombs made it impossible to know where you could go to be safe, except perhaps right out into the country. For Lucy's family, that wasn't an option.

He was still in the privy when he heard the drone of aircraft again. He straightened his clothes hurriedly and stepped out into the yard. He knew he should run for the house.

Yet, somehow he couldn't make himself move. He stared up at the grey-orange sky, watching the beams of the searchlights slicing through the smoke.

This was history happening right above him. He thought of all the black and white photographs he'd seen, and the bits of old film with planes silhouetted overhead. Now he was about to see it in colour, for real, just as he'd seen the Great Fire of London! He would be the only person ever to have seen the Great Fire *and* the Blitz with their own eyes!

He only had to wait for a few seconds. The planes must have been much closer this time. He wondered absent-mindedly why he hadn't heard them sooner. Perhaps he was slightly deaf from the explosions. All the same, standing right beneath them, their engines were thunderous.

They were flying in formation, just like in all the pictures. Shrieking whistles came from clusters of tubes showering from a plane over to the left. Joe turned his gaze to the plane on the right. The same whistling incendiaries were tumbling from this one too. The symmetry was oddly pleasing.

Then, out of the sky just ahead, he saw something larger drop. A parachute flapped open. Joe watched the parachutist drift down, calmly, slowly beneath the planes. It was either incredibly brave or extremely stupid to jump out of a plane right in the middle of a raid, he thought.

Abruptly, Lucy was yelling at him.

Joe swung round towards her voice. She stood in

the open back door. Then he realised what he'd just seen. The object beneath the parachute had been much too large to be a person.

The next moment, the sky split apart with the loudest noise Joe had ever heard.

Lucy flew through the air towards him. Joe was lifted from his feet and thrown backwards. Something flat, about the size of his hand, was spinning towards him. Light glinted on one side. It reminded him of a circular saw.

The ground slammed against his back, but he couldn't tear his eyes from the whirling disc. It must be a piece of glass. In a split second, it would carve straight through him.

He clapped his hands over his face and waited.

11

Perhaps he passed out. He wasn't sure. All he knew was that he'd been lying on his back, but now he was sitting on a chair. He was doubled over, his head on his knees as though he was dizzy or sick.

Now that he thought about it, his stomach *was* churning. The world seemed to be lurching to a standstill around him. He could hear voices and distant music. After the explosion, everything had gone silent for a moment, as though his ears had closed up against the onslaught of noise. What he was hearing now didn't fit. The music – it was the wrong music.

Even before he opened his eyes, he realised what must have happened. This was his world again, not Lucy's.

He should have felt relieved, this time more than ever before. Rationally, he knew it was good not to be lying out in Lucy's yard with glass flying through the air towards him and German bombers overhead. But he wasn't ready not to be there! The hissing in his ears that should have warned him must have been drowned out by the planes and the explosion. It had been so sudden too, the force of the blast so powerful! Lucy had seemed to leap out of the doorway. He gulped. Had he just witnessed her death? He clenched his teeth and willed the thought away.

"What on earth are you doing?" Dad's voice broke in. "Did you drop something?"

It took two full seconds for Joe's brain to realise that Dad was talking to him. He looked at the ground beneath his feet. It wasn't the ground, it was the floor of the tiered seating of the football stadium. His St. Christopher had fallen out of his bag and dropped through a gap.

Panic swept over him as he tried to think whether he'd left it behind with Lucy. She'd refused to take it. What had he done with it after that? He couldn't remember.

Then it came back to him: he'd dropped it into his coat pocket, then taken his coat off before he squeezed in under the stairs. Thank goodness he hadn't put the coat on when he went outside, or it would have come back with him!

He guessed he'd vanished in front of Lucy, which was probably a good thing, though she might not have actually seen, given the way the blast had flung her off her feet. As long as she'd survived that though, she might at some point remember what he'd said about the St. Christopher. Hopefully, she would find it in his coat.

"Joe?" There was a note of concern in Dad's voice. "Are you okay?"

"Fine," Joe mumbled. He spied his water under Sam's seat. "My bottle fell out, that's all."

He retrieved it and sat up again. The football pitch was empty. Some of the seats around the stadium were empty as well. It was half-time, he remembered.

The rest of the match passed Joe by. Nick and Sam leapt to their feet several times, and jumped about in a frenzy when a goal was scored. At the end of the game, Joe found that Liverpool had beaten Sunderland 2-0. He must have missed one of the goals altogether.

"You're very quiet," Dad said, as they made their way out of the ground. "I thought you were enjoying it in the first half."

"I did enjoy it," Joe said. "It was great, all of it was great!" He tried to summon a convincing amount of enthusiasm.

"But …?" Dad prompted

"But nothing! That first goal was amazing, wasn't it?"

Dad's eyebrows went up. "The second one was more impressive, didn't you think?"

"Oh, yeah. The second one was cool!"

They walked on, a few paces behind Nick and Sam, who were still jabbering about the match. It felt weirdly remote to Joe. He looked around at the houses they passed. On some streets, there were long sections of terraces, just like in Lucy's time. Most streets, though, had bits of newer housing of different ages and styles, from the 1950s up to the present. He wondered whether they were filling gaps left by the raids. Surely not all of them!

"Didn't Liverpool get quite badly bombed in the Second World War?" he asked Dad as they walked along.

Dad grinned. "Honestly, Joe! We come here for the football, and within minutes of the match ending, your historical antennae are waving around again! You're even more of a history nut than me these days!"

Joe looked at his feet. "I just remembered something we did about the Blitz at school. I know that was mostly London, but Manchester and Liverpool were hit too, weren't they, because of the docks and stuff?"

"I think so. Nick!" Joe's father called.

Nick paused so that they fell into step together. Now that they were away from Anfield, the streets were growing steadily less busy.

"Do you know much about World War Two in

142

Liverpool?"

"I'm not an expert," Nick said, "but I do know that the worst of it was May '41. The docks took a pounding and so did the areas next to them. Something like seventy percent of the buildings in Bootle were damaged or destroyed in the Blitz."

"Seventy percent?" Joe echoed. *124 Benedict Street, Bootle.* Seventy percent was almost three quarters. He gulped.

"The whole of the city centre was pretty much flattened," Nick went on. "Most areas have been rebuilt, some of it more than once. That's why the centre of Liverpool feels so modern. But there's an old church known as the Bombed Out Church that's been preserved in its ruined state. It's quite interesting. We could go there tomorrow if our young history fanatic would like to."

Joe saw Sam roll his eyes. "What about 1940?" he asked, ignoring his brother. "Were there many raids then?"

Nick thought for a moment. "The end of November was quite bad, I think. I remember reading that Liverpool had one of the worst civilian incidents of the war, so Churchill said. Something about people sheltering in the basement of a college. They should have been safe, because the ceilings were reinforced. But when the building was hit, the furnaces burst and boiling water poured down inside. People were burned alive, scalded by the water and steam, as well as buried in the rubble from the building above." He made a face. "The authorities did their best to get everyone out – not just the survivors, the bodies of the dead too – but after a few days, they had to give up. They poured lime into the basement and sealed it up to stop disease spreading from the remains of people rotting down there."

Joe shivered.

"That's horrific!" Dad said. "What a way to die!"

"It's like some medieval nightmare, isn't it?" Nick agreed. "Much worse than if you were in your own home. At least if your house took a direct hit, you probably wouldn't know."

Joe glanced at his uncle. It was uncanny to hear Nick speak his own thoughts from just a couple of hours ago.

"Was it just November, the bombing?" he asked.

"There was some in December as well," Nick said. "Two or three consecutive nights, I think. They're known as the Christmas Blitz."

"What dates was that?" The question shot out.

Joe's uncle looked at him, surprised. "I can't remember. We'll look it up when we get back later if you want."

Joe fell silent as they walked on. That was the

best thing to do, he thought. He would borrow Dad's laptop and look up which nights had been the worst raids. He wouldn't be able to take a list with him back into Lucy's time, but he ought to be able to commit the dates to memory. He might even be able to find out which areas were hit on which nights. He'd have to make a guess about how far forward to go from November. He should probably include May 1941, just in case, but the most important dates were almost certainly the Christmas Blitz.

Once he'd got the information together, he'd just have to hope Lucy called him back quickly enough for it to be useful. He realised he hadn't had the chance to tell her how to do that, but hopefully she would think of him when she found the St. Christopher. If he thought of her as often as possible, that might be enough. After all, it had worked long ago in Fishbourne, when neither of them had known what made it happen.

Of course, there was still one further hurdle: even if Lucy called him back quickly enough, *and* he remembered the information, *and* she believed it, would she be able to persuade Ellen to take action? It was hard to see where they could go.

"Come on, Joe!" Dad called. "You're dawdling!"

Joe looked up. Dad was waiting on the pavement some way ahead. Nick and Sam had gone on, no doubt still wrapped up in their analysis of the football.

Joe hurried to catch up with his father. He had the uneasy feeling that he'd let him down somehow, by so obviously losing interest in their long-awaited trip to Anfield. He was just trying to think of something to say to make it better when he heard the screech of tyres behind him.

On instinct, he turned towards the noise. A car had mounted the pavement. It was speeding straight towards him! He felt Dad's hand on his arm.

The car hit them.

Joe saw the sky swing round. He took in the light reflected off the windscreen, the bonnet passing below him, a tree still with leaves in the garden of the house next to him.

Disbelief flooded his brain. He couldn't have survived a bombing raid, only to be killed by a car on a pavement! *Not yet!* he yelled inside his head. *I have to help Lucy get through the war!* The ground soared up and hit him.

Darkness swirled through Joe's head. Bright points glittered here and there, like gems in black velvet. *So this is what it means to see stars,* he thought.

Or was he dead? Was this where you went when

you died? If there was no afterlife, it could be like this – whatever was left of you, floating in the nothingness of space. Except that weightlessness shouldn't feel this heavy! His limbs ached, his ribcage had been crunched. Cold came from beneath him.

He opened his eyes. It was daylight and he was sprawled awkwardly on his side. Rough flagstones sparkled with frost beneath him. He shifted himself. The air smelled of coal smoke. Hurriedly, he sat up. He was in Lucy's back yard.

A movement at the kitchen window caught his eye. He jerked his head round. Pain shot through his neck. Had it been the blast that had left him so sore? Or the car hitting him? The two things might feel quite similar. He blinked.

Who was that in the house? The glass of the window was criss-crossed with tape which hadn't been there before, making it hard to see through. He didn't dare crawl closer. There was no good reason he could think of for being out here, so if it was Ellen or Lucy's Aunt Jane, it would be much better to hide before he was noticed. Then he might be able to return to the house in a more plausible way.

Then he recognised Lucy behind the window. Her eyes were stretched wide and she was gesticulating frantically as though trying to flap him away. He glanced over his shoulder. She must mean him to go and hide in the privy. He got to his feet and stumbled over to it, pushing the door closed behind him.

He wondered what time it was. From the frost and the light, it seemed like early morning. The water in the loo had a crust of ice over it. Joe rubbed his arms with his hands and hoped that Lucy would come out soon. He had no coat, only this ridiculous sleeveless jumper, and the same shorts and long socks as before.

It was some time before the back door opened, however. Joe had been driven to jumping up and down and trotting on the spot as best he could in the tiny space, to stop himself from getting any colder.

But as Lucy opened the privy door, her face was worth the wait. "How on earth did you do that?" she cried.

"What?"

"I was washing up the breakfast things and suddenly, there you were, lying out in the yard!"

"Did you see me disappear too, during the raid? Wait, can we go indoors before we talk about this? I'm frozen!"

"Okay. Ma's gone out now." She led the way back into the house. Joe went at once to the kitchen fire and huddled over it. The warmth was blissful.

"Where's everyone else?" he asked.

"Peter and Pa are at work."

"And the others? Your uncle and aunt?"

For a split second, she looked confused. Then she said, "They've moved back home again. You've been gone three weeks, you know. Where've you been?"

"Back in my own world," Joe said, "though hardly for any time at all, less than two hours. It's a bit frustrating actually. I was going to find out which nights are going to be the worst raids and where not to go, but I haven't had the chance."

She frowned. "Why did you come back if you weren't ready?"

"Because it's not just down to me! You called me back, and because I was thinking about you, it worked."

"You were thinking about me?" Her cheeks turned pink.

"Of course I was!" Joe said impatiently. "I'd only just left you, in the middle of an air raid! I'm just glad you weren't hurt." *Or killed*, he added silently. "Did you see me disappear?" he asked again.

She shook her head. "I'd come out to find you – you'd been so long – and I thought I saw you standing there. I yelled at you to come in, but the next thing I knew, I was lying on my face and you'd gone."

"What happened?"

"A bomb landed in the road outside. Our front door and windows blew in. The blast went straight through the house."

"Did you come looking for me?"

"After that?! No way! I just crawled back into the house. The bombers were still going over. I spent the rest of the night under the stairs with Ma and Peter."

"You all survived the raid, then? Your father as well?"

"Yes, thankfully. It went on most of the night. The worst we'd had until last night. After you didn't come back in, we were really worried. Peter wanted to go out and look for you when it went quiet for a bit, but Ma wouldn't let him. And now you turn up again, talking as though no time has gone by!"

"Like I said, it hasn't for me. You brought me back really quickly."

"I didn't!"

"You must have done. Is that my St. Christopher round your neck?"

Lucy blushed. "I found it in the pocket of your coat." She pressed it between her thumb and finger. "If you must know, I was sorry you'd gone. When I found it, I decided I'd wear it to remember you by." Her cheeks turned a deeper red. "I suppose you'll be wanting it back now," she added.

"Not yet," Joe said. "I was trying to give it to you, remember, when I told you where I really came from. I wanted you to have it, to borrow it at least, because when you touch it and think of me, if I'm

150

thinking of you at the same moment, it brings me back to you."

He waited for her to declare this idea absurd, but her eyes shone. "That's lovely," she said. "So it connects us by our thoughts." She looked straight at him, and her gaze seemed to cut right through, as though she could read his deepest and most private feelings.

It was his turn to blush. "Well ... er ..." He cleared his throat. "Yes. Anyway. I hope I won't disappear again for a while, but we need to come up with a story to explain where I've been, if you think your mother will take me in again."

Lucy cocked her head to one side. Joe thought she was pondering the question, then realised she was listening. She made a face. "We might have to think on our feet," she whispered.

Joe heard the front door shut.

"That was quick," Lucy said, going out into the hallway. "Did you get everything? Let me take that." She came back into the kitchen carrying a basket.

"It's only half of it," Ellen said. "I'm so tired this morning, I forgot to take the ration –" She broke off. "Well, I never!" she exclaimed. "What is Joe Hopkins doing back here?"

151

12

"Hello, Mrs Lucas," Joe said quietly. The manner of Ellen's greeting made him wish the ground would swallow him up. "I'm sorry to turn up again like this. I didn't know where else to go."

"Really?" Ellen frowned. "You seemed to know where to go during the raid! I know we're not your family, but didn't it occur to you that we might worry about you? How could you leave like that and not tell us?"

"I was an idiot," Joe said. He didn't have to try to sound miserable: it came naturally. He hated the fact that he'd upset her again when she'd always been so kind to him. "I know you said it might not be long before the next wave of aeroplanes came over," he said, "but I didn't quite believe it. I wanted to see for myself what the place looked like in the middle of a raid."

"You went out? Through the back gate between

the yards? If you were that curious, why didn't you just go out the front door?"

Joe hung his head. "I knew you'd tell me not to."

"You're right! And with good reason!"

"I know that now. I was in the street when the bomb fell."

Ellen was still frowning. "I can't believe you were so stupid!"

Joe studied his hands. "I must have got knocked out," he mumbled. "When I came round, I was in an ambulance. That's why I couldn't tell you I'd gone."

Lucy's mother narrowed her eyes. "You haven't been in hospital all this time, though!"

"Er … no." For a moment, Joe floundered. Then inspiration came to him. "My uncle and aunt found me. They'd seen the article in the newspaper and tracked me down. They took me home with them."

Ellen swept the ration books from the table into her shopping bag. "Even so," she said, "you might have thought to let us know where you were, and that you were safe!"

"I did think of it!" Joe cried. "I thought about you all the time I was gone." He was glad to anchor his lies to a piece of truth. "I wanted to come back and see you." He hesitated, then plunged off into untruths again. "The thing is, my aunt and uncle live a long way from here, on the other side of the city. I can't remember the name of the district," he added, before Ellen could ask, "but I knew it would take too long to walk here and back without my aunt finding out. It's my uncle who's family, my mum's brother. My aunt is a strange woman – she didn't want me to go out at all."

"You could have written to us," Ellen pointed out. At last, her voice was less sharp.

"I couldn't remember your address." Joe knew this was feeble. Lucy had given it to him for the letter he'd sent to his mother, and he'd come and gone from her house several times.

Lucy clearly thought the same because she said quickly, "Joe's uncle and aunt's house was hit last night. His uncle was killed and his aunt's in hospital. That's why he didn't know where to go. Please can he stay with us again?"

Joe shot his friend a look of gratitude. Ellen was looking at her too. "Is that so?" she said. "Then why didn't he say so straight away?" She turned on Joe, her eyebrow arched. "I'd have expected the death of your uncle just last night to be at the front your mind, not an afterthought!"

Joe blushed to the roots of his hair. "I'm sorry. I didn't know where to start. I'm not sure I've really taken it in yet. It's all been so confusing!" He felt like a mouse being watched by an owl.

"Please can he stay, Ma?" Lucy pleaded.

Ellen didn't answer.

Joe shuffled his feet. This was more painful than ever before. "I understand if you don't want me here," he said, "but even one night would help. I really am sorry I was so stupid. I should have listened to you."

"I need to think about it this time," Ellen said. "I'm going to go and finish the shopping now, with the ration books, which I'm guessing you still don't have! Perhaps you might wash your face while I'm gone. You're very dirty."

The front door closed behind her, though not with a slam, Joe was relieved to hear.

"She'll come round," Lucy said, taking the kettle from the cooker and pouring water into a large china bowl. "She's just tired. We all are." She gave him a piece of soap and a flannel. "Last night's raid was even worse than the one when you were here."

Joe washed his face and the back of his neck. "You said three weeks have gone by," he said, "so it must be almost Christmas."

Lucy snorted. "It doesn't feel like it, but yes, it's the twenty-first of December. Ma's been saving coupons for weeks to try and get everything for a proper Christmas dinner."

But Joe's mind was elsewhere. "Was there a raid the night before last?"

"No." Lucy took the flannel and rinsed it under

the tap, then hung it over the fire to dry.

"Oh no! That means there'll definitely be one tonight, and maybe another one tomorrow. I wish my uncle had been more specific!"

"Your uncle?" Lucy sounded surprised. "Does he exist, then? I thought you'd invented him along with the rest of your story!"

Joe bit his lip. "I hated lying to you, Lucy!" he said. "I always hate it. I *do* have an uncle in Liverpool though, a real uncle, not the one you've just killed off." He grinned ruefully.

"I thought that was quite good!" she said.

"I did too, though I'm not sure your mother believed us."

Lucy wrinkled her nose. "No, I don't think she did. Where is this uncle, then?"

Joe rolled his shirt sleeves back down. "He lives in a flat in the Georgian Quarter. We're staying there at the moment. That was what gave me the idea for inventing an uncle, though Uncle Nick isn't married, so there's no strange aunt. There wouldn't be one anyway – if he ever does get married, I'll have another uncle."

"How?"

"Because he's gay," Joe said, puzzled by her incomprehension.

"Gay as in happy?"

Joe laughed. "No, gay as in he prefers men to women! Only he doesn't have a partner at the moment."

"But that's illegal!" Lucy's bewilderment had turned to shock. "Men go to prison for that!"

"What?" Joe's smile faded. "For having relationships with other men? How on earth is that a crime? It's not as though it hurts anyone!"

"It says so in the Bible! The church says so. The law says so!"

Joe shook his head. "Not in my time, fortunately. At least, not in Britain. Anyway," he tried to get back to the point, "Uncle Nick said the Christmas Blitz was two or three nights. This must be it!" He went to stand beside the fire again. "It means you've definitely got another night of heavy bombing to come, maybe two."

"Why do you say, 'you'? Aren't you staying?"

"I will if I can. I do want to."

Joe watched Lucy empty the bowl of water down the sink. Her shoulders had slumped as though she was depressed. Of course, you would be, he thought, knowing you had another sleepless night ahead of you cowering under the stairs with a real risk that you might be dead by the morning. For some reason, he didn't share the feeling this time. The war seemed more remote now that he'd been back to his own world. This was her war, not his.

All the same, he might be able to make it better for her. "I wondered if there's anywhere we could all go for the night, outside the city?"

"Like where?" Lucy's voice was flat. "People were doing that in September, driving out of town and camping in the countryside. But we don't have a car, and we'd freeze if we spent the night outside at this time of year, even if we could find a tent. No, we'll just have to stay here and hope for the best."

She rinsed and dried the bowl, then put it away and got out a pair of scissors. "I told Ma I'd make some Christmas decorations this morning, try and brighten the place up a bit," she said with determined cheerfulness. "We're not having a tree this year," she went on. "Pa said we should do without, and you couldn't put it in the front window anyway because of the blackout. We've collected all this though, so I was going to make streamers and paper chains."

Joe looked doubtfully at the pile of black and white newspaper on the table.

"There's some whitewash we can use to cover the words, and I've got coloured paints, so we can make them look nice. Don't look like that! It'll be fun!" She handed him the scissors. "Why don't you make a start while I fetch the paint and glue?"

Joe sat down at the table and began to cut strips.

He hadn't made paper chains in years, and he soon found it was more interesting doing it from scratch rather than using a kit. He and Lucy made stranger and stranger shapes, trying to outdo each other, and with the colours over the top of the white, the results were surprisingly effective.

Presently, Ellen returned from shopping. She still looked weary, but she was much less grumpy than earlier. "I managed to get some raisins," she said, "and the butcher slipped me some extra fat for dripping. Our Christmas dinner might be quite tasty after all." She put the shopping down in the corner. "Will you still be with us then, Joe?" she asked, both eyebrows raised this time.

"I hope so!" Joe said. Realising that didn't sound right, he said hastily, "I mean, yes, please, if you'll have me."

"Alright." Ellen's tone was still guarded. "You can stay, as long as you do as you're told and don't go wandering off!"

"Of course!" Joe nodded vigorously. "Thank you!"

"There's one other thing I've been thinking," Lucy's mother went on. "It's about our shelter under the stairs. I thought it was strong enough after your father nailed up the telegraph poles, Lucy. But I've just heard the Mumfords in Bianca Street were killed last

159

night, in the same spot in their house, with the same reinforcements."

Lucy winced. "It does happen. We've always known that."

"I was thinking, maybe we should go to one of the communal shelters if there's another raid tonight."

"Joe says –" Lucy stopped. Joe knew she'd been about to say there would definitely be a raid. He was glad she'd caught herself in time.

"What does Joe say?" Ellen replied irritably.

"Lucy and I were talking about the same thing," Joe filled in quickly, "because of my uncle and aunt's house. I'm still not sure it's better to go to a shelter, though. What about that one that was hit when I was last here, the college?"

"Durning Road." Ellen looked grim. "It's true, that was horrifying. Maybe we should stay put." She changed the subject then, and they talked about Christmas, and other things, until Peter and William came in for lunch.

It was Saturday, Joe discovered, and this week, Lucy's father and brother both had the afternoon off. The minute William walked in through the door, Joe felt uneasy. Lucy's father had always been a fair man, but Joe was sure he disapproved of him this time. It stood to reason that William might think he'd been partly to blame for Lucy discovering the unexploded bomb; and the worry he'd caused Ellen when he vanished wouldn't have made him any more popular. One way and another, he was glad when William banished everyone from the parlour after they'd eaten, so he could have his afternoon nap in the armchair.

Joe, Peter and Lucy helped Ellen carry the plates into the kitchen.

"I saw Tobias from the greengrocers down at the docks again this morning," Peter said. He leaned against the doorpost while Ellen started washing up. Lucy stood ready with a tea towel, and Joe had been looking around for another one. At Peter's remark, however, he pricked up his ears. From the stillness of the cloth in Lucy's hands, she was listening too.

"Tobias Hunt? Really?" Ellen said.

Peter nodded. "Someone said he's after a job that'll exempt him from call-up. I heard he'd been up to see Penrose. When I saw him though, he was talking to some official-looking government man. What the pair of them were doing down there, I don't know."

Lucy turned her head slightly. Joe caught her eye, but neither of them spoke.

"By the way," Peter continued, "I heard some sad news this morning. You remember that nice black sailor who came for supper here, Amos whatever-his-name-was? His ship was torpedoed by the U-Boats. He's missing, presumed dead."

161

Joe's heart stopped. Dead? Amos? That meant drowned. His skin went cold at the thought.

"That's terrible!" Ellen said, looking round from the sink. "He was married, wasn't he? Florence, I think his wife was called. And they had children, too, a boy and a girl. How sad!"

A lump blocked Joe's throat. Of course, people had died in the war. It was what wars did! But of everyone he'd met in Lucy's worlds, it shouldn't have been Amos! Amos had been strong and brave, and fiercely honest. If anyone deserved to live, it was him!

"A waste of a good man," Peter was saying.

"What about what he'd found out," Lucy asked, "about what was going on down at the docks, the thefts of cargo and all that?"

Her brother shrugged. "I'm not sure he'd got enough information, or found anyone willing to listen, come to that. All the same, I bet there are a few people who aren't sorry he's gone."

"What about the other stuff –" Lucy broke off, catching Joe's warning look. Peter wouldn't know anything about information being passed on, and they had no actual evidence of it yet, though Joe knew the government man would turn out to be Morley.

What if Amos had confronted Jackson and Tobias about what they were doing, he worried. They might have gone straight to Morley and told him when

Amos' ship was due to leave and the route it would take. If Morley *was* a spymaster, he could have passed the information on to the enemy. If that was true, this wasn't just another British ship that had been sunk: this was murder! Amos had been deliberately silenced!

Neither Joe nor Lucy said anything further until they reached the park after lunch, and were sure of not being overheard.

"Do you think that's what happened?" Joe asked her, when he'd told her his fears.

They were sitting on the swings again, not swinging this time, as the chains were too cold to hold. "If it is, we'll never prove it," she said. "I mean, suppose you're right, and this man is a German spy, he's hardly going to admit it, not to us or to anyone else. And who would take our word against his? Nobody!"

"We can't just let it go, though!" Joe protested. "Amos was a good man! We owe it to him to find out what happened!"

Lucy kicked her feet back and forth. "I'm not sure we do," she said, "just because he brought chocolate. I know you met him once more after that, but even so …"

Joe chewed his thumbnail. He couldn't tell Lucy he'd met Amos before without getting drawn into the rest of it. It was too late now to tell her about all her other worlds.

"I don't understand why you care so much," Lucy said, "especially when this isn't your time! You said already that Britain is going to win this war. The death of one sailor, even a sailor we'd met, is just that – one person. Thousands of people have probably been killed already. What's another one?"

Joe could feel his fingernails digging into his palm. He made himself relax. This Amos wasn't actually the same person as the other one, he reminded himself. This Amos hadn't lived through slavery any more than this Lucy had lived through the Viking Age. Amos wasn't owed a better life because of what had happened to him a hundred and fifty years earlier. He was owed a better life because of the kind of person he was!

They went home as dusk fell. It was still only late afternoon, but Ellen was busy in the kitchen preparing tea.

"I thought we'd try to eat earlier today," she said. "Then we won't go hungry if the sirens do go off at six or seven. Lucy, Joe, could you collect some things together, just in case? Your father is on duty again tonight, Lucy, but he and I have agreed that this time the rest of us *will* go to one of the shelters."

Joe gazed at Ellen. Was this the decision that would kill them all? Or the choice that would save their lives? It might easily be either. It was frustrating to know that he could have found out what they ought to do, if only he'd had more time.

"We'll need blankets and cushions," Ellen said. "Bind them up as small as you can – there are a couple of belts in the wardrobe. We'll take the torch of course, and the playing cards. Lucy, can you also find a bottle to fill with water and dig out the box of ship's biscuits from the back of that cupboard?"

"Things aren't going to be that desperate, are they?" Lucy grinned.

"I hope not!" Ellen returned her smile. "I just thought we might be peckish at three in the morning. We'll be glad of them then. If not, we could always use them to make ourselves helmets!"

Lucy laughed, but Joe shuddered. A sense of foreboding had enveloped him like an icy fog. What if everything was not going to be alright? He knew this was the last of Lucy's worlds – at some point over the last few days, he found he'd accepted that. But what if it was going to be the end of Lucy herself?

13

Lucy was halfway through the washing up after tea when the howling of the air raid warning began again.

"Saved by the siren!" she cried, dropping the plate back into the water and drying her hands. "Thank you, Fritz!"

Ellen untied her apron and put on an extra cardigan. "You won't think that tomorrow, when you come back to a sink full of greasy dishes!"

Lucy raised her hands as though in prayer. "Please, dear Fritz," she said sweetly, "put off the job for me! A small bomb in the neighbour's yard should do it. Just blow the windows in again and fill the sink with glass!"

Ellen tipped water from a bucket over the fire. "I'm glad he can't hear you! Run and put out the parlour fire, Peter. Then let's go!"

She hustled Lucy, Peter and Joe into coats and

hats, and out onto the pavement. Each of them took a bundle of bedding, while she carried the basket of provisions.

"Which shelter are we going to?" Peter shouted over the siren. "One of the ones along here?"

Ellen made a face. "There's a shelter under the railway arches near Kirkdale I've heard is less horrible. Safer too, further from the docks. Come on!"

She set off at speed along the street with Peter beside her, and Joe and Lucy trotting behind. At least the moon was bright tonight, Joe thought. The trouble was, he couldn't see the ground in front of him over the cumbersome bedding roll.

His earlier feeling of foreboding hadn't gone away, but had settled on him like a cloak, heavier than ever now that the raid was about to begin. It was awful to feel so helpless! There was nothing at all they could do to guarantee their safety, including this mad dash to the shelter. Hundreds of tonnes of metal and explosive would shortly start raining down on Liverpool. At the end of it, people who were alive now would be dead. There was no reason at all why that shouldn't include Lucy. Maybe she'd only survived in the past so that she could be there to meet him in the next world. If that was true, there was no need this time.

Another thought occurred to him, even more terrible: maybe *he'd* always been pulled back to safety so that he wouldn't die in his own world. Only he'd been thrown here this time by the car hitting him. If he was about to die in real life, back at home, there was nothing to stop him dying here! In fact, it would have to happen! He would be killed here at the moment he died in his own world!

"Nearly there!" Ellen called over her shoulder.

Joe's blood rushed in his ears. He looked up at the sky, at the moon sailing peacefully through soft clouds. A bomber's moon, Peter had called it. There was no point being afraid. He was only guessing at what might happen. Tomorrow morning, they might emerge from the shelter alive and well to find Lucy's street untouched. In the meantime, he should try and think of something else, anything at all.

He glanced around. From every side road they passed, people were coming towards them, joining a line moving purposefully in the same direction, everyone obviously heading for the shelter. Joe looked over his shoulder. The stream of people continued behind them. Then he saw something that stopped his breath in his throat.

Dad.

Joe's feet faltered. He stumbled, caught himself, twisted round and looked again, expecting ... what?

Someone else. Someone who looked like Dad but wasn't.

Only it *was* Dad!

Joe's feet stopped altogether, planted themselves in the pavement as though he'd taken root. Someone barged past him, cursing. Lucy, too, was beyond him now, about to reach safety. Joe could hear the distant hum of the planes, but he couldn't move. He stood there immobile, pole-axed by disbelief.

"Dad!" His voice cracked with the effort of shouting over the wailing siren. His father seemed dazed, drifting among the figures hurrying along the road.

"Dad!"

He couldn't believe his father had heard him, yet their eyes locked together. In the moonlight, Joe saw the astonishment in Dad's face. His father started towards him, but he was still moving like someone in a dream. A family overtook him, then another and another.

"Dad!" Joe shouted desperately. He couldn't see his father any more. He broke into a run, ignoring the grumbling as he shoved through the oncoming people.

Behind him, he heard Lucy's voice calling urgently. She would have to wait. He would find her later. The most important thing was to reach his father, to bring him to the safety of the shelter.

Questions thronged Joe's mind. What on earth was he doing here? How had he got here? Had he planned to come? What did it mean? Why now, after so many other worlds?

He was some way past where he thought he'd seen Dad when the truth began to sink in. The thread of men, women and children had dwindled, but his father was nowhere to be seen. Joe turned a full circle, staring in each direction.

He had gone. Vanished.

Joe made his way slowly back, peering down every side street. The roads were suddenly empty. Joe heard the bark of a warden. He paid no attention. Could Dad have gone into one of the houses along the road? It seemed very unlikely. His father hadn't moved like a man who knew where he was going, and he wouldn't walk into the house of a stranger.

The air raid warden yapped again. The siren had stopped. Joe heard the first crump of an explosion, and then a second. Instinct told him he should run. He quelled it and kept walking steadily, determined to be thorough in his search. How could his father have disappeared? It didn't make sense! Had he imagined him? Had it been someone else altogether? Yet, as their eyes had met, there'd been no doubt!

The throb of engines filled the air now. Joe wished his hands were free to cover his ears. It was so hard to think over the noise! What if Dad had been sent here for some purpose, what if he was Joe's guardian angel, sent to lead him away from danger? Perhaps he was here to stop Joe going to the shelter with Lucy. If that was true, if it was about to get bombed, he had to try and get her out! Joe gritted his teeth. If only he knew what to do!

"Joe!"

He looked up.

Lucy was haring along the street towards him, straight past the warden who'd left his post and was bearing down on Joe. "What are you doing?" she cried. "Why weren't you with us?" She seized his arm. "Come on, for heaven's sake!" She hauled him back along the street.

"I saw my dad," Joe said, tripping over his feet in an effort to keep up. "I don't know how he came to be here, or why. Then he was gone."

"Tell me in a minute!" she gasped.

The planes were roaring now. Joe glanced up at the sky as he ran. The silhouettes of the bombers were right overhead, ploughing through the night in formation, just like before.

The air raid warden stood blocking their way. Joe expected him to collar them both and yell at them. But his eyes were fixed on the sky. "Bomb!" he bellowed. "Get down!"

Lucy and Joe only hesitated a moment. Then they threw themselves face down on the pavement. A second later, an explosion ripped through the air. Joe's ears seemed to burst open. The ground quaked, as though the earth's crust had splintered!

Joe felt his hair stream back as if he'd dived into water. The force of the blast flattened him against the ground as it raged past above. Behind it, bricks and glass showered down in a monstrous hailstorm.

Lucy was already scrambling to her feet. She tugged Joe's arm. He saw her lips moving, but he couldn't hear her. He jumped up, abandoning the bedding roll. "What?"

She put her mouth to his ear. From the feel of her breath, he knew she was shouting, but her voice was still faint. "Can't stay here ... doorway!" She pointed towards a shop just along the street.

Beside her, the warden was getting stiffly to his feet. His tin hat had been knocked off, leaving the top of his head oddly vulnerable. Joe picked up the hat and held it out. The man scowled at him. It was Mr. Tuffett, the butler from Tregaris, glaring at Joe now exactly as he'd glared at him then! Joe almost laughed.

The man's mouth was moving too, probably telling Joe and Lucy off for being out on the street. Joe shrugged. Being deaf wasn't altogether bad, as long as it didn't last.

Lucy grabbed him. She pointed again. Joe looked. One of the planes was scattering dark sticks from its fuselage. He could just make out the whistling. A moment later, the first one hit the road and burst into flames.

Lucy whipped round and began to run towards the shop doorway. A movement in the sky caught Joe's eye. A shape had detached itself from the next aircraft. The moment seemed to spin out as he watched it fall, not straight down but diagonally, as though it was trying to catch up with the plane. It was coming straight for them.

"Bomb!" he yelled, and threw himself down a second time.

The air was torn apart again. The blast thrust him forward. Joe smashed against the pavement. His forehead grated on the ground. His body felt like he'd been stamped on. The noise was excruciating.

This time, it took him more than a minute to get his breath back. He lay wheezing in the dull quiet of his deafness. It might have been peaceful, not hearing what was coming next. But the danger was too great! They had to get to the shelter!

He sat up painfully. Every inch of him felt as though he'd been pounded in a fight. A warm trickle down his cheek told him he'd been hit by glass or shrapnel. He didn't dare touch it. He didn't want to know how bad the wound was. The important thing was that he was alive, and still in one piece.

He looked around for Lucy and saw her curled up in the shop doorway ahead. He leapt up and ran to her. "Lucy!"

She lay on her side, her face buried in the crook of her arm.

Joe dropped to his knees and shook her by the shoulder. "Lucy!" he shouted again. She gave no sign of having heard him, but he couldn't tell if his voice had come out properly. He couldn't even hear if the aeroplanes were still flying over.

He wasn't going to look now. Instead, he looked at the ground around his friend. There was no blood as far as he could see, so she wasn't injured. That was good, at least, though his own face was bleeding freely now.

He squeezed her arm, gently at first then more firmly. Something about the way she was lying wasn't quite right. "Are you okay?" he yelled. "Are you hurt?"

She didn't answer or raise her head. Surely she must have heard him!

Joe felt the stirring of nausea, a sick dread growing in his stomach. "Lucy!" he shouted again, "Lucy, wake up!" This time, he shook her so hard that she rolled onto her back. Her eyes were open.

174

"Oh, Lucy! You're alright!" Joe touched her cheek. "I thought for a minute –" He broke off.

Her eyes were open, but there was a thin layer of grit on the surface of them.

Joe stared. Then he staggered to his feet and backed away. Your eyes weren't supposed to have dust on them. That was why you blinked, to clean them. He put out a hand to steady himself against the shop front.

Vomit filled his mouth. He turned away and was sick on the ground. It wasn't possible! He must be wrong. She couldn't be dead! In a moment, she would splutter back to life and sit up, groaning, just as he'd done.

He wiped his mouth on his sleeve and crouched down again. There must be some sign of movement, even just the tiniest bit as she breathed.

There wasn't. He stretched out a shaking hand towards her. Her fingers were freezing. That wasn't necessarily a sign, he told himself. It was a cold night. He touched her cheek again. It was cool. He put his fingertips to her lips, tentatively, as if afraid she would bite him. No warmth came from between them, no breath. The skin felt dry and dusty.

He straightened up. "Help!" he yelled, as loud as he could. "Someone, please help!"

"It's too late!" the air raid warden snapped from behind him. "If you hadn't been such a silly fool, wandering about out here, she wouldn't have come after you!"

Joe wheeled round. How had his ears cleared enough to hear Tuffett's accusation? A few moments ago, all sound had been muffled! He wished it still was if this was the alternative.

He looked down at Lucy again. Was it really his fault that she was here? He supposed so. But he was still battling against the truth. "It can't be too late!" he begged. "There's no blood. She isn't hurt! If we can just get her an ambulance ... "

Another bomb whistled through the sky behind them. Tuffett shoved Joe roughly under the cover of the shop doorway and crammed himself in after him. The warden stood astride Lucy's motionless form as though she was just a heap of sandbags. His uniform reeked of fried onions. Joe recoiled.

"Ambulances can only help the living," the warden shouted, as the roar of the explosion died away. "She's dead, lad. Shock waves from the blast." He bent down and closed Lucy's eyes. She looked as though she was asleep.

"But there's no blood," Joe repeated. His voice rose. "She can't be dead!"

"I've seen enough bodies to know a corpse," Tuffett said. "We're only lucky it didn't get us too! Who was she, your sister?"

176

Joe shook his head.

"Your girlfriend, then?"

Joe's throat constricted. Tears welled up behind his eyes. He gritted his teeth and blinked them back. He would not cry in front of this heartless old man.

But there were too many tears coming. He stumbled out of the doorway and away down the street, away from his friend and from what had happened to her.

"What do you think you're doing?" Tuffett bawled after him. "You'll get yourself killed! I'm not risking my life for you again, idiot boy!"

Joe blundered onwards blindly. His chest was racked by sobs. There was no thought in his brain of what he was doing. He just had to put some distance between himself and– He couldn't say it, couldn't even think the words.

The planes were still flying over, squadron after squadron. Bombs were falling everywhere. Joe felt the shudders of explosions, heard the shriek of the incendiaries, saw the fires springing up. Yet somehow, it felt remote from him.

He looked up through the blur. The sky, which had been a moonlit navy blue half an hour ago, was orange now. Someone up there, someone who was already miles away, had pressed a button and killed his friend.

177

He tipped back his head and howled. The noise that came out was scarcely human, a cry of animal pain and rage. It wasn't possible! This couldn't have happened! How could he still be alive when she was dead? There hadn't been the tiniest scratch on her!

"Come on!" he yelled, shaking his fists at the bombers. "I'm down here! Come and get me! Kill me, too! If you're going to take her, take me as well! I don't want to be here without her!"

14

The planes flew on. Perhaps the pilots couldn't see the figure ranting at them far below. Or perhaps he was just too small to bother with.

Joe waved his arms and yelled until he was hoarse. Lucy had said the Luftwaffe sometimes dived low and fired on people out in the streets during raids, but none of them seemed to feel like it tonight. At length, exhausted, he wiped his eyes and gave up.

A kind of numbness was creeping over him. It was true, he didn't want to be here without her; he didn't want to be anywhere. He should probably try to go home to his own world, but he couldn't think how to get there. Surely the danger he'd been in already should have catapulted him back. He wondered what it would take, but couldn't bring himself to care.

He trudged on. After a while, he noticed the sky was empty again except for the pall of smoke which lay over the city, thickest towards the docks. He wondered distantly whether Lucy's father was alright. Had he, too, been hurt or killed by a bomb? What about Ellen and Peter?

Joe's insides twisted together. They didn't know what had happened! Ellen would still be waiting for her daughter, watching the entrance of the shelter, hysterically anxious by now. Once she knew … Joe couldn't bear to think of it. And when she found out that Lucy had turned back for him … He felt a wrench of physical pain. She would never forgive him. There was nothing he could say that would make any difference, not even telling her how much he'd loved her daughter.

Fresh tears sprang in Joe's eyes. He'd known for a long time that he loved Lucy. Yet he'd never said it, not even to himself. He should have done! He should have told her before it was too late!

Too late. He wanted to sit down on the pavement and weep. But his breath hung in the air, and though he hadn't stopped moving since he left Lucy, his fingers were frozen, his toes stuck together in his boots. If he sat still, he would only grow colder.

He couldn't spend the whole night outside, he realised. He wondered where to go. He couldn't go to the shelter they'd been heading for, because Ellen and Peter would be there. Perhaps he should go back to Lucy's house, if he could find it. It would be warmer in her kitchen, or even under the stairs, than it was outside, and he wouldn't have to talk to anyone. That might be best, as long as he was gone by the time the family came home.

Except that Lucy's washing up would still be in the sink where she'd gleefully abandoned it. Fritz had certainly done as she'd asked. She would never have to finish it! Joe choked. He couldn't go back: her ghost would be everywhere, helping Ellen with the shopping, making decorations for a Christmas she wasn't going to see, standing at the sink blushing as she touched his St. Christopher.

The St. Christopher, he thought listlessly, she still had it. It didn't matter. After all, he would never need it again, not for travelling back into the past. As for the idea of it keeping its wearer safe … a yelp of bitter laughter came out of his mouth. What a spectacular piece of fraud!

He plodded onwards through the glowing night, passing fresh craters in the road, houses burning or newly ripped apart, a tram car lying on its side in the rubble.

Some time later, another thought occurred to him. Maybe the St. Christopher did still matter. After all, Lucy had always given it back to him just before he faded out of each world for the last time. Maybe he was still here now because he didn't have it. The pendant might be the key to going home, in the same way that it had been the key to getting here.

He stopped. Would he be able to find his way back to Lucy? He'd taken no notice of where he was going. He didn't even know how long he'd been walking. If he didn't try though, he'd never know. Besides, it wasn't as though he had a better plan.

He set off back the way he'd come. For the first time since the bomb, he had a faint sense of purpose: here was action he could take, something he could do. It wouldn't change what had happened, but if he could find his St. Christopher and get it to take him home, he'd be able to hide himself away in his own world. It would be better to grieve for Lucy there, instead of being doomed to wander through the wreckage of her life with nowhere to go and no-one to care.

It took him a while to find his way back to the right area. There were more people around now that the planes had stopped flying over. He passed air raid wardens and policemen, fire wardens running to and fro with buckets of sand and beaters, and firemen with hoses.

"You know the raid's not over!" someone shouted as he went past. "There'll be another wave soon enough. You need to get inside until the all clear!"

Joe hurried on, taking no notice. At last, when

he thought he must be close, he paused to ask directions to Kirkdale station. Ellen had been taking them to a shelter under the arches which probably wasn't too far from the station. From there, he could guess the way back to the shop doorway.

"Kirkdale?" The fireman he'd approached was aiming his jet of water into the parlour of a smart house. He looked round at Joe, causing the water to arc away. "You weren't going to the shelter there, were you?"

"No, no," Joe said.

"Just as well," said his colleague. "It took a direct hit tonight. We'll be on our way over as soon as we've put this fire out. It's all hands on deck to get the survivors out."

Joe's jaw dropped. "Survivors," he echoed soundlessly. That meant Ellen and Peter, if they hadn't been killed.

A shudder ran up his spine as he remembered the sense of foreboding that had come over him in Lucy's kitchen. Had he known in some deep part of his mind what was going to happen? He didn't see how. Yet he'd been right to be fearful! They should have stayed at home!

The one awful consolation was that if Lucy's mother and brother had died in the shelter, that meant Lucy would have died too if she'd been with them. So it wasn't his fault that she'd been killed.

At once, he felt ashamed. It was wrong to wish her family dead, just to be free of his guilt. He put his head down and pressed on in the direction the firemen had said.

When at last he found the place where Lucy had been lying, there was no sign of her. He looked around, bewildered. Where could she have gone? *How* could she have gone? Could it all have been a terrible mistake? Maybe Tuffett had been wrong! Maybe she'd just been unconscious, and now she'd come round and gone off somewhere!

"You lost something?"

Joe looked up. A man in a tin hat was shifting rubble away from a fire hydrant nearby.

"There was a girl here," Joe said. His own voice sounded unfamiliar. "My friend," he added.

"They took her away," the man answered, "a few minutes ago."

"Who? Who took her?"

"Ambulance."

"Then she was –" A crazy hope leapt in Joe's chest. *Ambulances can only help the living.* So she wasn't dead after all! She was going to be okay!

The man shook his head. "'Fraid not."

"You just said it was an ambulance!"

"They collect the dead too, on nights like this."

There was sadness in the man's expression. "She was just a kid, wasn't she?" he said. "It's everything that's wrong with this war! I saw a mother and her three little ones laid out last night, and there's other things I've seen, arms and legs and such like, I'll never forget 'til my dying day." He cleared his throat. "Your friend, was she? I'm sorry, lad."

Joe gaped at him. She *was* dead then. His chest buckled, as though punched by a leaden fist. He hadn't even said goodbye to her. He should at least have done that.

He sat down in the doorway where she'd lain and traced her outline as well as he could remember it. The St. Christopher would be gone with her, though that felt pathetically unimportant now. He'd been clutching at the idea of it for something to do. But what was the point in doing anything? When the next wave of planes came over, he might get killed anyway.

He drew his knees up and rested his head on his arms. He was miserably cold. Maybe he could just freeze to death, except that it would take too long.

As he heard the drone of the planes again, he got to his feet. He could dance about wildly in the street until one of them saw him and took aim.

He was about to step out of the cover of the doorway when something bright caught his eye. A heap of grit and glass was piled against the shop door,

185

as though washed up by the tide. Joe stooped down and pushed the debris carefully aside. It was probably just a piece of broken window.

But his fingers closed over a small silver disk, about the size of a ten-pence piece. He rubbed it on his sleeve. Against all the odds, he'd found his St. Christopher.

The pendant had just a few centimetres of chain left. The rest must have gone, along with the catch, when it had been blasted from Lucy's neck. Joe pressed it tightly against the palm of his hand, as though it could connect him to her again. The metal was ice cold.

He turned around. "I'm ready!" he called to the sky. "I'm ready to go home!" He stepped out into the road.

"Home?" came a drawling voice from nearby. "Home where? To our Father which art in heaven?"

Joe spun round. To his disbelief, Tobias was coming out of the house opposite the shop. A bike was propped against the wall. Tobias wheeled it into the road. "Are you hoping to sacrifice yourself?"

"What are you doing here?" Joe snapped.

"Me? You say that like we know one another. Have we met?"

"Not really," Joe growled. "Only once, at the greengrocers last month." He wondered if Tobias would remember him.

The young man pretended to think, then shrugged. "No. You obviously didn't make an impression!" He smirked. "As for what I'm doing, I could tell you, but I'd have to kill you!"

He swung his leg over the saddle of his bike. "Lovely to chat," he said sweetly, "but I need to get back to my vantage point, before that lot get here." He jerked his head towards the approaching planes. "They'll be adding plenty to the havoc their comrades have caused. Quite a good night they're having." He sounded pleased.

He lifted his foot to the pedal, but before he could set off, Joe leapt in front of him. This might be the only chance he had to find out what Tobias was up to with Morley and Jackson. Maybe there wouldn't be time to do anything about it, but if he knew what it was, he could at least try. Perhaps *that* was why he was still here. Perhaps he hadn't faded out because there was something he had to do, or something he had to stop.

He seized the handlebars with both hands.

"Get off!" Tobias shook the bike. "Do you want me to run you down?"

"You can't," Joe said, forcing the front wheel round so it was pointing to one side. It was liberating, not caring what Tobias did! He couldn't run Joe over with the bike, but he could punch him and knock him out cold. He could pull out a knife and stab him. The planes might reach them and bomb them. It was all the same to Joe. He had nothing to lose! "Tell me, what are you doing here?"

Tobias glowered. "As it happens, I was visiting a friend of mine. He's a very respectable gentleman by the name of Mr. Albert Morley, not that it's any of your business!"

"I knew it!" Joe spat.

Tobias' features froze for a moment. Then he recovered himself. "Knew what?" he asked in a bored tone.

"He's a government agent, isn't he?" Joe narrowed his eyes. "You're passing secrets to the enemy! You give him information, and he passes it on! You're traitors, both of you!"

Despite the darkness, Joe saw two spots of colour appear on Tobias' cheekbones. Whatever he'd expected Joe to say, it wasn't this.

The young man gave a forced laugh. It was probably meant to sound scornful, but the pitch was too high, enough to tell Joe that he'd been right.

"What gives you that idea?" Tobias sneered.

"Did you think nobody would notice?" Joe retorted. "Or did you just think you were cleverer than everyone else? Well, you were wrong! I've seen you talking to Morley, and I'm not the only one. I've heard whispers about not wanting to be called up to fight for the 'wrong' side, *our* side!" Joe took a chance. "I know about the shipping routes lined with U-Boats who've been forewarned, and about the aircraft parts being sabotaged. You're being watched, Tobias Hunt."

To Joe's satisfaction, Tobias' eyes flared in alarm. He glanced over his shoulder.

"So what is it you're doing now?" Joe went on. "Observing the raid from a safe place, so you can report back to the Germans which targets they hit?" He had no idea if this was right, but it was plain he'd been right about everything else. "Why not just wait for tomorrow's newspapers to fill in the picture?"

"Because there's a news blackout!" snarled Tobias. "Or hadn't you noticed? The press never reports what gets hit! The British government may be limp, but they do know they have to stop that information getting back to the Luftwaffe!" He snorted. "Unfortunately for them, the Nazis are one step ahead as usual. They've got plenty of us on the ground here, more than happy to help.

"It's pathetic, you know," he went on conversationally. "Churchill makes all these big speeches, but his pockets are as empty as his words! He can't do anything! What this country needs is real leadership, a bit of discipline, someone we can all believe in. We need what Adolf Hitler has given Germany!" A strange look came into Tobias' eyes. "Hitler has pulled Germany up by her bootstraps and the sooner he invades Britain, the better!"

"You actually want the Nazis here?" Joe was incredulous. It dawned on him that he hadn't given any thought to what Tobias was ultimately aiming for. He'd been too busy piecing together the first part. "You want Britain to become part of the Nazi state? You want to live in a country that tortures and kills people who don't fit the pattern? Disabled people? Homosexuals? Jews?"

"Who wants people like that? They're poisoning the country! Anyway, you don't know that's what he'll do!"

"Actually, I do," Joe said. "I know without a shadow of doubt."

"He's building a new world!" Tobias cried, as though Joe hadn't spoken. "A stronger, cleaner, better world, with a strong man to lead it! Hitler is a great thinker, but he's a man of action too. He showed that in the way he took France. And he's got Denmark and Norway, the Netherlands, Belgium, Luxembourg! There's no stopping him!" Tobias was almost falling over his words. "He's been generous, too, in the peace he's offered Britain. But no, this stubborn little island has turned him down. We've refused the best offer we're ever likely to get!"

"Thank heavens for that," muttered Joe. "And we'll hold out until we win."

All at once, a shaft of doubt pierced his certainty. What if *this* was why he was still here? Surely Tobias couldn't change the course of history on his own! But Morley might have connections who could. What if he and Tobias did something together that changed the outcome of the war? Joe couldn't think what it might be, but if there was even the smallest possibility, they had to be stopped!

"Britain deserves the battering she's getting!" Tobias raved. "I couldn't care less! I've made sure I'll be well rewarded when this country is part of the Third Reich!"

His eyes glittered. A muscle twitched at his temple, and there was a looseness about his jaw that made him look slightly mad.

Joe regarded him. Here was every Tobias from every one of Lucy's worlds, including Tiberius and Thorbiorn, all rolled into one! Here was the boy on the look-out to improve his standing. Here was the young man who always weighed up what he might gain. Here was the person who despised and feared anyone who was different to him. Here was the fanatic who would stop at nothing for what he believed in! If Tobias discovered some crucial piece of information that

191

could cost Britain the war, there was no doubt how he would use it.

"It won't happen," Joe said, through gritted teeth. "Germany won't win."

"Of course they will!" Tobias spoke with contempt. "Have you forgotten Dunkirk already? British soldiers scrabbling to get off the beaches! It was humiliating! And on the other side, the massed armies, the tanks, the aeroplanes, the people waving flags with the light of hope in their eyes! When did you last see anyone with light in their eyes here?"

The image of Lucy's sightless eyes sprang unbidden into Joe's mind. That light had gone out for good.

"You'll understand, I can't let you endanger my chances." Tobias' voice fell suddenly, ominously. He got off the bike. "Somehow, you've found out far too much. I doubt anyone would believe you, but it's a chance I can't take!"

He wrenched the handlebars free of Joe's grasp, and threw the bike aside. "Did you know," he hissed, "that since the Blitz began, the number of murders has soared? Every man who's sick of his nagging wife, every worker who's ground down by his boss, everyone who's ever hated anyone has got the chance to do something about it! All you have to do is drag the body into a ruined building, and people assume

192

they were killed in a raid."

He advanced on Joe, who took a swift step back. Clearly, Tobias meant to kill him. For himself, he truly didn't care as long as it was quick. But if he was still here because someone had to stop Tobias then he couldn't let that happen! He owed it to people other than himself to survive. He owed it to his own future.

What Tobias had just said went both ways too: if anyone had ever hated someone, he hated Tobias. Maybe now was the time! Maybe that was what he was here for – to kill his enemy at long last!

He swallowed. "I'm not the only one who's put two and two together," he said, trying to take in the idea. "You can get rid of me, but it won't stop the authorities finding you!" It was a brazen lie. Without Lucy and Amos, he had nothing.

"Maybe not," Tobias snapped, "but it's a start!" He loomed over Joe.

Joe stood his ground this time, watching Tobias' body language to work out what kind of weapon to expect. A blade of some sort, probably. If Tobias had a gun, he would have pulled it out already.

But before Tobias could move, there was a sudden scream of engines. A plane hurtled down out of the sky.

15

The air beat in Joe's ears. Through it, he could hear the judder of machine guns. He whirled round. The fighter plane was scarcely clearing the rooftops. It swept up the street towards them, its headlights dazzling. Above them, Joe felt sure he glimpsed the pilot in his goggles and flying hat, his face lit up by his instruments as he craned to look down on the road he was strafing.

All at once, Joe felt an immense surge of power. He had summoned this! These guns were firing because he had wished it. He forgot all about stopping Tobias or holding the course of history. All he wanted was to go home, and this was the answer!

Bullets bounced off the railings and ricocheted off the pavement. Joe watched them with mounting excitement. Any moment now, he would find himself back in his own world.

But it was Tobias who fell. Joe looked up as the

aircraft passed over, and then down, blankly, at the young man. It had happened so fast. He could hardly believe it.

From a hole no larger than a marble, a dark stain was spreading across Tobias' body. It was too far down to have hit his heart or lungs, but it might have got his stomach. Joe wondered coolly if the wound was going to be fatal. It would be fantastically ironic if Tobias was killed by a German!

Tobias clearly had the same thought. "Bloody idiot!" he rasped. "Bloody idiot, shooting at me when I'm on your side!" He shook his fist weakly at the sky.

Joe bent over him. "What was it you said, just a minute ago? If you die here, on the street, everyone will think you're just a victim of the raid." He stood back. "I could kill you. In fact, I probably should."

Though he spoke calmly, his heart had begun to pound. This was just the chance he needed. Maybe it was his destiny. But was he really ready to become a murderer in order to stop Tobias?

"You're just a kid!" jeered the young man. "You couldn't do it!"

Joe gazed down. Absolute confidence radiated from Tobias' face. His belief in his own superiority was unshaken as ever. This was the man who'd taken pleasure in pouring hot wax over someone, who'd been ready to do far worse. Joe remembered Amos' scars, inflicted by men like Tobias.

Something snapped inside him. "I might be just a kid," he said, his jaw clenched, "but I've seen my best friend killed tonight by the people you want to help! The world will be a better place without you!"

He cast around and picked up a jagged piece of glass from the ground. "I have more reasons to kill you than you could possibly imagine," he snarled. "Give me just one reason why I shouldn't!"

Tobias' throat moved. The confidence had seeped away. His mouth opened, but no sound came out.

Joe raised his glass dagger. He wasn't interested in hearing Tobias beg for his life. He didn't want to draw this out.

Then he hesitated. He had to do it right, so that it wasn't too obvious. If he plunged the glass into Tobias' neck, that should do it. Tobias would die quickly, and it would look like the glass had been embedded by an explosion.

But the blood! There would be a gruesome amount of blood! It would spurt everywhere, probably all over him, still warm. Joe felt sick.

He steeled himself again. If he didn't do it now, he would lose his nerve.

"I can give you a reason," said a man behind him.

Joe froze. He knew who this was without turning round.

"War may be murder on a grand scale," the man continued, "but that doesn't make it right to take another man's life, no matter what he's done."

Morley stepped forward and stood beside Joe. He wore the same long coat and hat as down at the docks, as though he was on his way to the office rather than venturing out in a raid. "Over here!" he called down the street. "There's a young man been shot. He needs urgent help!"

Joe looked up. Two men began to run towards them while a boy on a bicycle sped away.

Morley took the glass gently from Joe's hand. "No more of that," he said.

"No more?" Joe cried. "I should kill you, too! I know what you and Tobias are doing. You're as much of a traitor as he is!"

Morley blinked. "If you've found that out," he said mildly, "my young friend can't have covered his tracks very well!" He shook his head at Tobias. "Let's allow these men to look after him until the ambulance gets here. Would you like to come inside my house? It's warmer, and –" His words were interrupted by two explosions, one immediately after the other, some way off. "I was just about to say, safer than out here!" The engines had grown loud now. The fighter must have been ahead of the next squadron.

"I'm not going anywhere with you!" Joe snapped over the noise. "Now that I've found you out, you'll silence me, just like you silenced Amos!"

"Amos?" Morley seemed genuinely nonplussed.

"Amos Harper." Joe looked up. The planes were almost overhead. Maybe one of them would drop a bomb and kill them all, him, Morley and Tobias, in one fell swoop. That would tidy up the loose ends, Joe thought grimly.

"I don't know who you mean," Morley shouted, "but we really must continue this conversation somewhere else." He took Joe's elbow in a vice-like grip. "If you'd rather stay somewhere more public, this shelter will have to do."

He steered Joe towards one of the small brick buildings. Joe began to struggle, then stopped. What was the point?

Morley pushed open the metal door. Damp cold hit Joe's face. There was a second door. It clanged shut behind them. They stood in utter darkness. As Lucy had said, it smelled of pee.

Morley switched on his torch and shone it swiftly around the room. A bench ran the length of each wall, but there was nobody in here. So much for staying somewhere public! Joe edged away from him. He didn't rate his chances of escaping.

His captor wrinkled his nose. "It's probably for the best that there's nobody in here," he said, wiping the bench with his handkerchief before sitting down. "I'd like to get this done quickly all the same so I can get back to my own shelter. Tell me, who is Amos Harper?"

"Who *was* he, you mean," Joe replied sharply. "His ship was torpedoed just after it left Liverpool." He paused until he could be heard again over another explosion, nearby this time. "I saw you down at the docks collecting information," he went on. "So did Amos. The next thing I heard, his ship had been sunk by the German U-Boats!"

"I'm sorry to hear that," Morley said. He sounded sincere, but Joe wasn't going to be taken in. Morley's accent was that of an educated Londoner, out of place here. There was no way he was doing any kind of normal job around the Liverpool docks.

"You may be surprised to know that things aren't always what they seem," Morley said. "Since we can't be overheard here, I shall come straight to the point. You are correct in thinking that Tobias Hunt has been supplying me with information he thinks would be useful to the Germans."

Joe watched Morley suspiciously. He hadn't expected him to admit this so soon.

"I'm impressed you've worked that out," Morley

said, "and a little concerned at how careless Tobias may have been. If you've reached this conclusion, others may have done so too." He raised his eyebrows in an unspoken question.

Joe said nothing.

"I take it you believe, as Tobias does, that I'm a spymaster," Morley said, "collecting and passing on information to the enemy. I presume that's how you think I could be responsible for the death of your sailor friend. That is a relief, I must admit. It's imperative that my informants believe –" His words were cut off by a loud explosion.

"– believe that to be true," he resumed, when the building had stopped trembling. "I am no such thing, however."

"What?" Joe scoffed. "Do you think I'm stupid?"

"Clearly not," Morley assured him. "And it's fair enough that you don't trust me. In wartime, it's a good idea not to be too trusting. I don't trust you either, Joseph Hopkins."

Joe gasped.

"That is your name, isn't it?" The man made a small sound of satisfaction. "I make it my business to know everything that goes on on my patch," he said. "So I know that you came out of nowhere, disappeared and then reappeared again just as suddenly. That's why I don't trust you. I don't know how you did that, or where you came from."

He looked at Joe thoughtfully. "On the other hand, I know that you've been staying with Lucy Lucas, who was killed right outside my door tonight. I know who her parents are, and I know they're honest. They seemed to trust you, so perhaps I've been wrong not to."

Joe looked away, trying to avoid Morley's scrutiny. He'd been ready to loathe this man, not only for what he was doing this time, but for their last encounter too. Yet, it wasn't as simple as that. Moreover, Morley seemed to be suggesting that they were on the same side.

"I'm going to tell you something that *must* remain a secret," he said. "I cannot impress on you enough how important it is that you don't talk about this conversation to anyone! My work is critical to the war effort. If you breathe a word, the whole operation could be compromised."

"Who would I tell?" Joe shot back. "As you said, my friend is dead."

Morley nodded sympathetically. "We have to win this war, so that her death hasn't been in vain," he said. "Make no mistake, when I say 'we', I do mean Britain!"

He looked into Joe's face. "I am no spymaster, not in the true sense, though I do have a circle of informants. Tobias Hunt is one of them." He paused. "In any conflict there will always be some who want to help the enemy. They're often brave and determined, but they're also misguided, and they don't share the same priorities as their fellow countrymen." He sighed. "I wish it weren't so."

"But these people bring you information to help the Germans!" Joe was still belligerent. "Why, if you're not a spy?"

Morley ignored his tone. "Our prime minister has decided that the safest way to control these people is to seem to give them what they want: someone they believe is a double agent who will send their information to the enemy."

"That's what they think you do?"

"That's right. I've taken great care to make sure of that. You must admit it, my cover works. You were taken in, just like Tobias."

"So what do you actually do with the information?"

"I keep most of it in a drawer beneath my bed." Morley smiled. "Almost none of it leaves my house, never mind Britain! The thing is, if I didn't collect it from them, they would look for someone else. Who knows, maybe they'd find the real thing, someone who would actually pass it on! This way, at least we can guarantee their information never reaches the enemy.

We can find out quickly, too, if people like Tobias are getting close to anything important."

"And Amos' ship?" Joe was still struggling to adjust his view of Morley.

"Tobias and some of the dockworkers have certainly been feeding me information about routes and cargoes. But since everything they've told me is still in a bedroom just out there," he gestured to the door of the shelter, "it's simple misfortune that your sailor's ship was sunk. I'm afraid the U-Boats are already very good at what they do, without help from Tobias or the others. Until we have some way of cracking the code they use to communicate, our ships will have to keep running the gauntlet with what little protection we can give them."

Morley sat back. "Does that put your mind at rest?"

Joe thought for a few moments, then nodded.

"Very well. I'm going to go back now. I don't think I can bear to stay in here a moment longer! You're welcome to join me in my Anderson shelter for the rest of the raid if you wish. It's a little damp, but nowhere near as fragrant!"

Joe shook his head.

"In that case, I wish you well, Joseph Hopkins. And remember, never a word of what I've told you, not to anyone!" Morley switched off the torch, opened first one metal door and then the other, and disappeared.

Joe sat for a few seconds in the stinking darkness. He felt deflated, drained of his righteous indignation. He and Lucy hadn't been wrong, not about Tobias at least, nor about Jackson and Metcalfe. And since none of them knew the truth about Morley, it was no wonder he and Lucy hadn't discovered it either. It was pleasing, too, to know that Tobias had been confiding in someone who was deceiving him, and would continue to do so if he recovered from his bullet wound.

That didn't change the fact that he was still alive though, Joe thought savagely as he let himself out of the shelter. Tobias shouldn't have lived when Lucy had died!

He walked away along the road. How would he have been feeling now if Morley hadn't stopped him killing Tobias? Satisfied, maybe. More likely, horrified. There had once been a time when he would have killed Tobias with his bare hands. But the murderous rage that had driven him to that point had been absent tonight. If he'd done the deed this evening, it would have been because he thought he should, not because he truly wanted to.

Now, he was at a loss again. He looked up vaguely at the sky. There were still bombers flying over, though the explosions were more distant just now. The sky still glowed orange though, embers were still flung into the air from the fires all around, the smoke was still getting thicker. In spite of all this, the raid seemed to Joe more remote than ever.

He walked on, oblivious to where he went or how much time passed. At some point, the planes stopped again. Ambulances went by, and another couple of boys on bicycles. Joe's ears were ringing from the bombardment.

Presently, he thought he heard a child crying. He stopped walking and turned his head to listen. It was hard to be sure. His ears might be playing tricks.

The sound came again. He crossed the road towards a ragged gap in a terrace. He'd passed countless houses like this, some bombed tonight, some last night or before that. How long this house had stood in ruins, he didn't know, but he began to climb over the rubble towards the noise.

It was definitely a small child weeping. Joe started to lift the slates and timbers, throwing them in a heap to one side. The front of the house had collapsed, bringing the roof down in a landslide over the smashed walls. It was heavy work and his hands were soon scuffed and bleeding. Some of the roof was too big for him to move. Joe worked his way carefully around the trapped timbers and clusters of bricks. The family would probably have been downstairs, maybe under the stairs like at Lucy's house. If he could clear a way into the bottom of it, he might be able to get the child out even though he couldn't lift everything off the top.

Sometimes the crying stopped. Joe worked harder than ever then. Having got this far, he couldn't bear the thought of reaching the child too late. There was no other sound from the ruin, no other voice or sign of movement. That meant this little boy, if it was a boy, had already lost everything: his home, his parents, his brothers and sisters. Joe could not let him die alone down there!

As he worked, he found himself remembering a line from a film about the war: 'Whoever saves one life saves the world entire.' That was what he would do. Tonight had been more horrifying than his worst nightmares, but if he could save this one life, this child might have a future it wouldn't have had without him.

Joe laboured on, fighting the exhaustion that was beginning to slow his movements. Sometimes he called out encouragement to the child buried below him. Once he asked his name. No answer came back. It went quiet for a very long time. Joe hoped the boy had stopped crying because he felt comforted to know Joe was there, working to free him.

Another wave of bombers arrived. Still Joe

carried on. He couldn't hear anything now over the engines, the fearsome whistling, and the explosions. It seemed odd to think he'd been crouching under the stairs with Lucy and the others last time. Tonight, so many planes had flown over his head without hurting him, he was starting to feel invincible.

At last, he saw a tiny gap appear in the rubble at his feet. He dropped to his knees and began hauling stones and bricks away. *Let him be alive!* he prayed. *Please, please, don't let him have died, or be horribly injured.*

The gap grew larger, a dark hole like a cave beneath the ruin.

"I'm here!" Joe called. "I've nearly got you. Just a few more minutes!"

Suddenly, he saw a hand reach out, small and grubby. Then another hand stretched up towards him. This one was caked in blood. Joe flinched at the thought of what he might be about to find. At least the child was alive though.

And she was a girl. When he finally lifted her out, her long hair was full of dust but she seemed mostly unhurt. Joe sat down heavily on a beam and cradled her in his lap. Her face was filthy except for the clean tracks of her most recent tears.

For a while, they sat together, cuddled close, not speaking. The planes had gone again leaving the night eerily quiet.

Then Joe felt the little girl stir in his arms. She looked up at him, her eyes clear through the mask of dirt. "Where's Mummy?" she asked.

Joe swallowed. "I don't know," he said. "What's your name?"

"Evie. What about Margaret and Lillian? Where are they?"

"Are they your sisters?"

She nodded.

"I'm afraid I don't know about them either. How old are you?"

She looked down. "Four," she said, counting her fingers. Then she noticed the other hand. "I've got blood!"

Joe smiled. "You have, but it's not bleeding now, is it? It's all dry. In a minute, we'll go and find someone to clean you up. You'll be fine."

"You've got blood too!" She put her fingers up to his cheek. "That's ouchy!"

He laughed. "It's not too bad. I'd forgotten all about it, actually." He looked along the street. "There are some people down there who can help us. They'll take you somewhere warm."

"What about Wilfred?"

Joe's heart sank. Another child killed. "Who's Wilfred?" he asked. "Is he your brother?"

She gave a peel of laughter. "No, silly! He's my toy dog!"

"Oh!" Joe grinned, at least partly in relief. "I think we might have to come back for Wilfred later."

Evie's face crumpled. "I don't want to leave him! I want Wilfred! Please can you get him for me!"

"Okay, okay!" Joe stroked her head. "Let me take you along to the first aid man, then I'll come back and find Wilfred."

She looked unconvinced. Joe was unconvinced, too. He'd never find a toy dog in all this, and he'd likely find much worse. Then inspiration struck. "You know, actually I think I saw Wilfred earlier. He was going off to help some other children just like you, by digging them out. But he said to give you this to keep you safe while he's gone." Joe fished his St. Christopher out of his pocket.

Evie's eyes lit up. "That's pretty. Can I keep it?"

"I think that would be very nice," Joe said. He put the St. Christopher into the little girl's hand and closed her fingers over it. "You make sure you look after it now, and it can look after you." He lifted her into his arms and stood up.

The air swirled with smoke as he picked his way back across the ruins of Evie's house to the road. "Do you want to walk?" he asked, when they reached flat ground.

"No, you carry me." She put her arms round his neck.

Down at the end of the street was an ambulance. A group of people were busy around it, tending the injured, bringing out the dead.

Joe set Evie down as they reached it. At once, a woman in uniform bustled over with a blanket and put it round Evie's shoulders. "You sit down there, my dear, and get warm. In a moment, we'll check you over. Maybe we can even find you a sweetie to make you feel better. Would you like that?"

Evie nodded.

"I've just got her out of the house up there," Joe said, pointing back along the road.

The woman stood up. "Is there anyone else?" she asked, her eyes sliding towards Evie and back again.

"She mentioned her mother and two sisters," Joe said.

"And Wilfred," the little girl piped up.

"And Wilfred, the toy dog," Joe added, "though as I told you, he's gone off on a mission to save other children." He looked at the woman. "I couldn't hear anything." He shook his head deliberately.

"I understand. We'll see what we find. In the meantime, let me clean up that cut on your face. It looks deep. If you don't get some stitches in that soon, you're going to have a nasty scar."

Joe put his hand up to his cheek. One last scar, he thought, and one that he was going to have trouble explaining away when he got home. Because all at once, he knew he *was* going home. Maybe it was Evie, maybe saving Evie's life somehow made up for Lucy.

Or maybe it was just time to go, at last.

He shook his head. "I'll get it seen to later," he told the woman. He crouched down in front of Evie. "You look after that silver circle, won't you?" he said. He squeezed her hand. "It's actually a necklace, but it needs a new chain. Maybe someone will give you one."

"Are you going now?" Her eyes were bright and innocent.

"I'm going to go and help Wilfred," he said. He reached out and stroked her hair. "Take care of her," he said to the woman.

Before she could answer, he turned and walked away into the dark fog that rolled up the street towards him.

16

It was light in the room, Joe could tell that before he opened his eyes. He lay listening to the sounds around him: voices a little way off, a metal clinking as something was wheeled along, a quiet, steady beep.

It was remarkable how tired he felt even though he'd only just woken up. His head ached too, and his limbs were sore. It might be a good idea to drink some water.

He opened his eyes. He was in a white box of a room. Hard, white ceiling, hard, white walls. Glaringly bright. He closed his eyes again.

"He's awake! Nurse, he's waking up!"

He knew that voice. It was Dad. He'd spoken softly, but Joe could hear his excitement. The room dimmed beyond Joe's eyelids as someone bent over him. "Joe, can you hear me?"

Joe sighed inwardly. The darkness had been

peaceful. He wanted to stay there, where he didn't have to think, but the way back seemed to have closed.

He tried to touch his face. His arm felt stiff. There was something taped to the back of his hand.

His fingertips reached his cheek. The skin was smooth, flat, exactly the same as it had always been. There was nothing to mark where the gash had been. No scar.

He held up his palm in front of his eyes. It took him a moment to focus. He blinked. No scar there either. He closed his fingers over where it should have been. It had definitely gone.

"You're awake!" Dad's face beamed down at him. "Back in the land of the living!"

Joe burst into tears.

It was amazing how much he missed his scars, he thought, as he sat at the table at Dad's house nearly a month later. Even now, he still found himself tracing the line that used to run across his palm. They'd all gone, all six of the scars he'd brought back from Lucy's worlds, as well as the one that never was, on his unblemished cheek. That would have been very obvious, unlike the rest. It was probably just as well he hadn't had invent a story to explain it. Given the choice between that, though, and losing all seven, he knew what he'd have preferred.

It was the one on his palm he missed most, the one Lucy had made with the penknife. He hadn't had it very long compared to some of the others; but because it was on his hand, he'd looked at it every day. He remembered running his finger over it in class while he was thinking, and stroking it as he gazed out of the window on the bus. It had been such an important part of him, its disappearance hurt almost as much as the cut which had caused it.

"You remember I've invited a few people over this evening?" Dad said, coming into the room.

Joe looked up from his homework. School had said he didn't need to worry about catching up until after the holidays, but he knew that the longer he put it off, the worse it would be. He hadn't planned to do too much this afternoon, which was just as well. He'd scarcely managed even half of it. Maybe his teachers had guessed how hard he would find it to concentrate.

"You know most of them," Dad was saying. "The Penningtons are coming, and the Johnsons and Millers. Gill and Rex are coming too, with Kasper."

Joe nodded.

"The thing is, I've invited someone else as well. Not just one person actually." Dad rubbed the back of his neck. "I realise this isn't the best time to tell you, but there hasn't been a right time. I was going to tell you last week, but –" He stopped mid-sentence. He was floundering, Joe realised. What on earth had come over him?

"You see, it's just that, well –" Dad took a deep breath. "I've met someone else, another woman." He went on quickly, "Of course, your mum is still your mum. That'll never change. But I've been seeing this person for a while and I thought it would be nice to get us all together, with it being Christmas and all." The words were tumbling out now. "Maybe I should have cancelled, after your accident, but I arranged it ages ago, before we went to Liverpool. It's always so hard to find a date close to Christmas when everyone's free. I thought it would be a good time to have her over with her kids – I haven't met them either – you know a sort of casual get-together for mince pies and mulled wine or whatever …" His voice trailed off, like a wind-up toy that had run down.

"That sounds nice," Joe lied. There was something both hopeful and helpless in the way Dad was behaving. Seeing him so uncertain made Joe feel embarrassed.

It was daft really, because he didn't mind Dad having someone else. For a while after his parents had split up, he'd hoped the separation was temporary, that they'd sort out their differences. Over the last year, however, both of them had clearly been building new lives, and both of them had seemed happier and more relaxed than they'd been for a long time. Joe knew Mum had been going out on dates, too. She hadn't said anything about them, and she'd arranged them for

215

when he and Sam had been at Dad's, but he'd heard her on the phone to her friend. He wondered about telling Dad this, but decided against it. It would make things more awkward, not less!

The real problem was that Joe didn't want to do anything or see anyone. As far as he was concerned, Christmas should be cancelled, certainly this year, maybe every year. He wanted to shut himself up in his room and put some music on, and think about Lucy, or try not to think about Lucy, or do whatever the hell it was you were supposed to do when someone you loved had died.

A lump thickened in his throat.

"You don't mind then?" Dad asked anxiously.

"Mind?"

"Me being with someone who isn't Mum."

Joe shook his head. Tears were welling up behind his eyes. He turned away. If he cried, Dad would think it was the new woman, when it was nothing to do with her.

The grief rose up and broke over him like a wave. He gulped. This kept on happening! He'd think he was fine, and then suddenly, he wasn't. In the middle of breakfast, or while he was watching TV, or lying in bed, he'd find himself felled by the knowledge that he was never going to see Lucy again. Each time, the pain was as sharp as ever, as though he hadn't already faced it over and over! He didn't know how he would ever bear it.

He saw in his mind's eye again the crooked way she'd been lying. His fingertips still carried the touch of the dust on her lips. Worst of all had been her eyes, looking out through that frosting of grit, unseeing.

She'd looked otherwise unharmed, that was what made it so hard to take in, curled up in the doorway, her heart stopped by the blast. He still couldn't believe it. Even Tobias had been bleeding, Tobias who'd probably lived to see another day! It was all wrong!

Joe stifled a sob and fought his despair back into the tight little space inside him.

"So it's alright if they come this evening?" Dad asked doubtfully, "because I could put them off, I could put everyone off, if you'd rather. I hadn't done anything about it yet because I was waiting to see how you were. I thought maybe a bit of distraction ..." Once more, his voice trailed away.

"It's fine," Joe lied again. The evening obviously meant a lot to his father. He couldn't very well say no, even though he'd much rather not see anyone. He concentrated on breathing smoothly in and out. The wave of grief ebbed. He knew it hadn't gone, but at least it had receded for now.

He forced himself to think about the evening. He liked all the other people who were coming. The trouble was, they were bound to make a fuss about how brave he'd been about the accident, even though as far as they knew, he'd just bounced off a car. He *had* been brave, he supposed, or determined anyway, digging that little girl out of the rubble while planes dropped bombs around them. But no-one here would ever know about that.

As for meeting Dad's new friend, there was nothing to be gained by putting it off. Having to be polite to total strangers was hard work at any time, especially when those strangers included someone who might one day become your step-mum. At least, if she came this evening and it all got too much, he could make his excuses and sneak off to bed. Nobody would hold it against him if he didn't feel like being sociable.

"There's just one other thing," Dad said. "A bit of a complicating factor, I suppose you might say, after what you mentioned in hospital."

Joe looked up. He didn't remember very clearly what he'd said in hospital. Dad had referred to it a couple of times, but Joe hadn't dared ask.

"It's silly really," Dad went on. "Of all the things I thought might cause a problem, I never thought…"

"What is it?" Joe cut across him.

Dad grimaced. "It's her daughter. I'm afraid it might be quite hard for you. It's just an unlucky coincidence. Although … you know what, maybe I should put them off, have everyone else this evening, but leave inviting them until the new year. I should have thought this through."

"What? What's the matter?" Joe knew he sounded snappy, but really! Why couldn't his father get to the point?

"Her daughter has the same name as that friend of yours who died," Dad said. "I know how upset you've been about that. It's always such a shock when someone you know dies, especially when they're young."

"You mean the girl who's coming is called Lucy?" Lucy … Lucy …. The name seemed to ring in the air.

Dad nodded. He was watching Joe almost fearfully, bracing himself for another outburst of misery.

But Joe felt a kind of rumbling inside him. Was it possible? He hardly dared give shape to the hope that was forming in his mind, let alone put it into words. Lucy was dead, he told himself harshly. There was no going back. It was over.

Yet, that knowledge slid out of his brain, pushed aside, like earth shifted by some unstoppable force trying to break out of the ground. Something wild was drawing itself together in his chest, getting larger and larger, ready to erupt.

Joe found he was on his feet. He shook his head. There was a roaring in his ears. Yet it wasn't the roaring he was used to, the rush of time changing. This was a tumult of possibility and mad, desperate hope.

He clung to the edge of the table. This was ridiculous! He'd lost the plot! There *was* no hope. There couldn't be. It was just coincidence, meaningless unlucky coincidence, like Dad had said.

All the same, a question formed itself on Joe's lips. He held it back a moment until he could speak lightly.

"What did you say your new girlfriend was called?"

"Girlfriend!" Dad pulled a face. "I think we'd both prefer 'partner'!" He was clearly relieved that Joe hadn't got upset again. "Her name's Ellen," he said.

"And her son? Her other child is a boy?" Joe could hardly get the words out.

Dad frowned. "How did you know that? You're right, though. He's called Peter."

By the time the doorbell went three hours later, Joe felt wrung out. While he'd showered and changed, his brain had worked frantically through every loop and knot of the situation. It was so hard to take in!

He'd wondered, as he stuck a fresh dressing on the last remaining wound from the accident, whether Lucy might be impressed by his injuries. She'd never been noticeably impressed by that sort of thing before, but her reaction might have been more typical of her other worlds. If she was like a lot of girls now, she might be like the ones at school who cooed and clucked whenever someone got hurt. He winced. Let her not be like that!

What if she was, though? He agonised as he helped Dad get the nibbles ready and make the place look nice. What if she was only interested in clothes and make-up and posting selfies on her phone? Even if she wasn't boring in that way, she might not like any of the things he liked. What if she didn't like books? What if she wasn't interested in history? What if she loathed the sort of music he liked? What if she loathed him? She wouldn't, would she? Joe didn't feel sure.

There would be the whole thing about him knowing her as well, and her not knowing him. He'd had to endure that conversation over and over, and every time he'd hated it! Was he really going to have to go through it again? The good thing was that this *would* be the last ever time! Even as he thought this, he remembered consoling himself with the same idea only a few weeks ago. This really would be the last time though, no question.

But as he tried to imagine the exchange between them, he quailed. No-one from his own time would believe he'd met them in a past they didn't remember! It would be much better not to tell her. He hadn't told her everything in the most recent world after all, only that he'd come from the future. Moreover, this time he wouldn't have the kinds of problems he'd always had in the past, of saying or doing the wrong thing because he didn't understand her world. He wouldn't vanish in front of her either.

No, he decided. With both of them on home ground here, the best thing would be to start from scratch becoming friends. One day, when she'd had time to get to know and like him – if she *did* like him – then he might tell her. If he waited until then, perhaps she would believe him.

His father had believed him after all, although now he thought about it, Joe wasn't sure whether he'd mentioned the bit about the past. He furrowed his brow. He'd come round in hospital all bandaged and covered in tubes, and like an idiot, burst into tears. Something about what had just happened to him had obviously spilled out before he'd got himself under control, because he'd told Dad about Lucy. He'd probably told him the truth, too, since he'd been past caring about hiding it any more. But had his father understood she was from another time? Or had he just thought she was someone from school, and dismissed the rest as nonsense?

Joe looked across the hallway at his dad. The sound of the doorbell faded in the air. Dad's eyebrows were drawn together.

"Here we go, then!" his father said, putting on a smile. "Of course, it isn't necessarily them, though I did suggest they might come a little earlier than everyone else. I assume she'll have brought the kids. That was the idea, though it's always possible that something else has come up."

They both looked at the front door. *What if she hasn't*, Joe thought. *What if she's come without them?* He longed to be able to bore through the door with his eyes. Was Lucy on the other side of it, about to walk into his world? Or was he going to have to wait until another day?

The doorbell rang a second time.

"Are you both going to just stand there?" Sam had come out of the sitting room. "What are you waiting for?"

The rest of my life, Joe answered silently.

Dad stepped forward.

Joe held his breath.

His father opened the door.

17

Three figures stood on the doorstep, wrapped up against the December night. But Joe only had eyes for one. "Lucy!" Without meaning to, he stepped forward and put his hands out.

Lucy's eyes widened. The colour drained from her face.

Joe shrank back, cursing himself. Why had he done that? She would think he was really weird, greeting her so warmly when she'd never met him before! What a stupid thing to do!

All the same, he couldn't get over the fact that it was her! *His* Lucy, not dead! Not lost forever! Best of all, here! It was so astonishing! So wonderful!

"That's quite a welcome," Ellen exclaimed, "for Lucy, at least!"

Joe turned scarlet.

"I hadn't realised I'd be playing second fiddle to my daughter like this," she said, with a laugh. "I guess it's something I'll have to get used to as she grows up."

Ellen's hand stretched out towards Joe. He shook it, unable to meet her eye. "I'm Ellen," she said. "You must be Joe. This is Peter."

Beside Joe, Dad was shaking hands with Peter, introducing himself and Sam.

Joe stole a quick look at Lucy. Her colour had returned, her cheeks rosy from the cold, but her eyes were still wary.

"Come in, come in! It's bitter out there!" Dad drew Joe back into the hall to allow their guests to enter.

"Are we early?" Ellen asked. "You did say seven, didn't you?"

Lucy shivered as she pulled off her hat and scarf and smoothed down her hair. She was wearing a bit of make-up, Joe was startled to see. She was in trousers for the first time too, jeans, with a top that was much more flattering than any of the drab, ill-fitting clothes she'd worn when they'd last been together. Her hair was long now, and gleaming. He found himself marvelling at how well she looked, as well as how pretty. He could scarcely take it in that she was here, alive and real! Even better, she wasn't about to be snatched away from him, or rather he from her, after just a few days!

She glanced up and caught his eye. At once, they both looked away. Her expression of shock seemed to have subsided. Joe thought she looked puzzled.

225

He shuffled his feet. "It's nice to meet you," he mumbled.

She nodded. "You, too." She didn't look at him, and didn't say anything else.

Joe bit his lip. Maybe she was quiet because she thought he was creepy and didn't want to talk to him. He swallowed. It mattered, this time it really mattered, that she should like him. Yet somehow, they'd got off to a worse start than ever before, except perhaps the time he'd met her in Bristol.

"Come on through." Dad led the way into the sitting room. "The others will be here fairly soon, but I thought it might be good to have a few minutes with just us. Do help yourselves to nibbles. What can I get you to drink?"

Joe hovered beside the door as Dad took requests. Lucy was standing close to Ellen, but she wasn't looking at her mother. She seemed preoccupied. Maybe there was somewhere else she would prefer to be right now.

It wouldn't be with her father, that much Joe did know. He'd died three years ago, Dad had told him, while he'd been showing Joe pictures of Ellen on his phone. Joe hadn't made any comment on the photos. There was no way he could say that he knew Ellen! It had been strange enough as it was, seeing her cheek to cheek with Dad.

How would Lucy feel about Dad replacing her father, he wondered. Had her dad been William? Joe couldn't help pondering the logic of it. Lucy had died in the last world, and here she was with Ellen and Peter, who had almost certainly died as well. Was William not here because he'd survived there? If that was true, Joe realised, he should be glad that Tobias hadn't died on that awful night. The last thing he wanted was for Tobias to turn up here!

Nudged by Dad, Sam was offering round a bowl of crisps. His brother's shoulders were hunched, Joe saw. He seemed to be finding it all as excruciating as Joe. For a second, Joe felt a flash of sympathy with him, before he noticed Sam watching Lucy with a hungry look in his eyes.

Joe spun round to look at her. She hadn't seen, though Ellen had clearly spotted Sam's interest, judging by the way the corners of her mouth twitched. Joe swung back to his brother, outraged. Lucy was *his* friend! Sam had no right to be looking at her like that!

He picked up a plate of mince pies, choking back his fury. Helping Dad an hour ago, he'd imagined himself gliding round the room with the nibbles, making amusing remarks while Lucy looked on with shy admiration. How had it gone so wrong so quickly?

Dad came back with a tray. "Mulled wine for us," he said, handing a mug to Ellen, "and four cokes for you adventurous lot." He gave one each to Peter and Lucy. Joe put the mince pies down again and watched the bubbles bursting on the surface of his drink. It was all a disaster.

"Joe?" Dad's voice broke in on him. "Ellen just asked how you're doing?"

"How I'm doing?" Joe was confused.

"After the accident?"

"What accident?" Peter asked.

Ellen waited for Joe to answer. When he didn't, she said, "Joe was hit by a car when he was up in Liverpool at the football last month."

"Really? What happened?" Peter sounded eager.

"A car drove up onto the pavement," Joe said. It wasn't something he particularly wanted to talk about, but it was better than staying locked in mortified silence. "I flew over the bonnet," he added, "and woke up later in hospital. I was lucky, though. Nothing broken, no internal damage as far as the doctors could tell, and the bruising's better now. It's only really this left." He touched the dressing on his temple. "I hit something sharp on the pavement. They put some stitches in but it got infected so it's taken a while to heal. They said I'll probably have a scar." The last word caught in his throat.

He looked at Lucy, longing to tell her about all the scars he had lost, and the part she had played in each one. It wasn't possible, he saw abruptly, that they could ever become close unless he told her the truth.

"What was it like, being unconscious?" Peter asked. "I've heard people sometimes have strange dreams, like seeing a light at the end of a tunnel."

"You're thinking of near death experiences,"

Ellen said. "I don't think Joe was nearly dead."

Joe felt Lucy watching him. He remembered her actually dead. The bomb that had killed her could just as easily have killed him. In a way, he *had* had a near death experience.

He hesitated, then said lamely, "No, nothing like that."

The doorbell rang. "I'll get it!" He escaped from the room.

His bedroom door opened in the darkness a few hours later.

"Are you still awake?" Dad bent over Joe's bed.

"Yes."

The mattress moved as he sat down. "I'm sorry about this evening," he said. "It was too much for you, wasn't it? I thought you seemed up for it when we were getting ready, but the doctor did say it might take longer than you'd expect before you were fully recovered."

Joe didn't answer.

"Anyway, I just wanted to say thank you for letting me go ahead with having everyone over. They were nice, weren't they, Lucy and Peter? I really liked them."

Joe coughed to cover a sob.

"Did you not? What's up?"

"It was her." He swallowed. Then it came out in a rush. "Dad, it was her! Lucy! She was my Lucy, my friend who died!" He felt tears racing inside him, tears of grief still for the friend he'd lost, and of disappointment for the friend he hadn't found. "She doesn't know me. I expected that. She's never remembered me from one world to the next. But I couldn't connect with her in any way! I've always managed to win her round quite quickly before!"

There was a pause. "The Lucy who died?" Dad repeated cautiously. "From one world to the next? What do you mean?"

"From all the times in the past!" Now he'd begun, Joe was desperate to tell someone everything! Two and a half years was long enough to have kept this secret! "I thought I said, when I was in hospital, about going back into different times in the past and always meeting Lucy."

There was another pause, longer this time. "Yes," Dad said slowly. "At least, you told me where you'd just been, and what had happened there."

"Did you not believe me? Is that it? I know how crazy it sounds, but this is her!"

"I do believe you," Dad said quietly. "And I believed what I could understand of what you told me in hospital."

"Didn't I explain?"

"You were babbling rather, so I didn't realise there'd been other worlds. But I understood what you were saying about the world I'd seen for myself."

It was Joe's turn to be silent. Then he said, "The

one you saw? So it *was* you!"

"Yes, it was me. Was that really you there too?"

Joe scrambled to sit up in bed. "What happened? How? Where …?" He couldn't even get the questions together. There was too much to ask.

"I've been thinking about this a lot, and I still don't really get it." Dad shifted his weight. "The car that hit you clipped me too, I think that's what did it. I grabbed your arm just before it hit you, so it got both of us."

He cleared his throat. "It wasn't anywhere near as serious for me. I banged my head on the pavement, but that was all. I blacked out, but not for long. Uncle Nick called 999 and by the time the ambulance got there, I'd come round. In the short time I was unconscious though, I had a really peculiar dream, a little like what Peter was asking you about earlier on."

Joe was glad of the darkness. This conversation would have been inconceivable in broad daylight.

"At least, I thought at the time I was dreaming, although it didn't feel like it. I felt as though I was wide awake." Dad paused again. "What's interesting is that I'd had a few moments like it before, years ago. Until this happened, I'd forgotten all about them."

"What was the dream you had when the car hit us?"

Dad put his hand over Joe's. It was warm and strong. "I dreamt I was back in the past. I assumed it was still Liverpool, though I couldn't be sure. There were no street names or other signs, and the road was nothing like the one we'd been on in the present.

"It was night, and really dark. The street lights weren't on, but then the moon came out from behind the clouds. There was an awful noise, a siren of some sort blaring, and people hurrying past me."

Joe nodded.

"I was bewildered. I didn't know where I was or what to do. I decided I should probably follow everyone else. I knew it must be urgent because of the siren, and because the people were all in a rush. But I couldn't seem to move very quickly – you know how it is when you're dreaming. And then I thought I saw you." He stopped.

"You did!" Joe cried. "It *was* me! I saw you too! I ran back along the road. But you'd disappeared. Where did you go?"

Dad was still. "I only just recognised you, you know. You weren't wearing your normal clothes, were you? You looked like a boy from that time, the Second World War I presume. What were you doing there?"

"I was on my way to the air raid shelter with Lucy. I was so excited to see you! I really wanted to get to you! Then you vanished and Lucy came after me. That was why we were both still out in the open when the first planes came over." He hesitated. "That was how Lucy was killed."

"I'm sorry," Dad said quietly. "Her death was my fault, then."

Joe shook his head. "It wasn't." Another thought occurred to him. "In fact, you might have saved my life! The shelter where we were going got bombed. I think Ellen and Peter were killed. I would have been killed as well if we'd all been together, and Lucy would still have died."

"Ellen and Peter?" Dad's voice was full of wonder. "So you know them already, too? That's how you knew she had a son? My goodness!"

Joe chuckled. "I couldn't very well say anything, could I? 'Nice to meet you, Mrs Lucas. How do you like my world?' Anyway, what happened to you? Were you just thrown back into the present for some reason?"

"That's exactly how it felt!" Dad exclaimed. "I suppose it was because I woke up, or came round. At any rate, I was back in our own time, about to be picked up by the ambulance. It was so short, the dream, probably only a couple of minutes at most."

"It was enough for you to believe me though," Joe said, "when I started telling you what had happened."

Dad shrugged his shoulders in the dark. "It might not have been. I might have assumed you'd just had the same experience as me from being hit by the same car. Sort of parallel dreaming." He rubbed his forehead. "But then while I was lying there on the hospital trolley, while they checked me over, I remembered the other moments I'd had like that in the past."

"When you'd been knocked out?"

"No, it had never been that dramatic before. It was after my mother died, your Nain. You were very young. You probably don't remember her."

"I remember her singing to me, a Welsh lullaby."

"That would have been Suo Gân." Joe heard the smile in his father's voice. "She used to sing so beautifully. I'm glad you remember that."

"That's the Welsh for you!" Joe laughed. "You've always said it!"

"That's certainly true. Though as it happens, she wasn't Welsh, not by blood anyway."

"Really?" Joe was taken aback. "But she spoke Welsh, didn't she? And we always talk about her as Nain, just like we call your dad Taid."

"She was evacuated to Wales during the war – from Liverpool, actually. I'd forgotten that. She must have been a very small child at the time. The Welsh couple who took her in adopted her. She never left."

"What about her family?"

"They were killed. A bomb fell on their house. It was a miracle she survived. She arrived in Wales with nothing."

Joe's heart skipped a beat. "Nothing at all?"

"Only a doll given to her by one of the firemen, and your St. Christopher."

Joe's hand went to his neck, where the pendant

used to hang. "You never told me it was a family heirloom."

"Didn't I? I suppose I had other things on my mind when I gave it to you." Dad shook his head. "The story goes that it was clutched in her hand when they pulled her out of the rubble."

"I don't have it any more," Joe said softly.

"No, I thought not. I was fairly sure you'd have had it with you in Liverpool. I suppose the chain got broken in the accident, did it?"

"No. No!" Joe's voice bubbled with something like laughter.

Dad turned his head. "Why's that funny?"

"It isn't!" A sudden joy was surging inside Joe. "That's not how I lost it." His head whirled. "It was my way into the past! It was the St. Christopher that did it, that took me there, to all those different times. I used to leave it with Lucy, so she could call me back."

"I don't understand."

"I'll explain in a minute. The thing is, she was wearing it when the bomb fell. I found it in the ruins, after they'd taken her away." He blinked at the memory, still powerful even though he'd seen her alive again this evening. "I thought it would bring me home. In every other world, I always faded out just after she gave it back to me. But this time, nothing happened.

"I didn't know what to do. I was wandering through the city in the middle of the air raid, thinking maybe the danger of the bombs would throw me home, when I heard a child crying."

"Go on," Dad murmured.

"It was coming from the ruins of a house. I began moving the bricks and stuff."

"On your own?"

Joe nodded. "It took a long time, but eventually I got to the child and lifted her out. She was unhurt. I couldn't believe it! She was four years old, she told me. Her name was Evie."

There was utter silence. Joe had the feeling his father was trying to get control of his emotions.

"She was sad about a toy she'd lost," Joe went on. "I knew she'd probably lost her whole family. I gave her the St. Christopher to distract her. It was the only thing I had."

"Did you know your Nain's name was Evelyn?" Dad asked quietly.

"Yes!" Joe's joy bubbled up and over. "It all makes sense! You see that?"

"I can hardly take it in! You saved your grandmother's life!" Dad shook his head in disbelief. "If you hadn't done that, she would have died. I would never have been born and you would never have existed. It's an impossible circle!"

"In a way, yes. But there's something else, too. You see, in every other one of Lucy's worlds, I had to put right something that was wrong. Quite often, it was something that had gone wrong because of me. Once it was done, once things were right, I faded out."

Dad nodded.

"Until now," Joe continued, "I couldn't see what I'd done in Liverpool to make a difference. I thought perhaps it was that I'd saved a life to make up for Lucy's death. Somehow, that didn't feel like enough though. I didn't realise it had anything to do with the St. Christopher. I gave it to Evie because she had nothing, and because I knew I wouldn't ever need it again to travel back in time and see Lucy." Joe heard the wistfulness in his own voice.

"Yes, but in doing that, you put it into the hand of the person who would one day pass it to me, to give to you."

For a while, they sat in silence, contemplating this.

"Those moments I mentioned before," Dad said presently, "the dreams, as I thought they were, they happened after your Nain died, when I got the St. Christopher.

"She'd left it to me in her will, quite specifically. I thought at the time it was a little odd, but I assumed it had particular sentimental value for her. After we helped your grandfather clear out some of her things, I brought it home with me and wore it for a while." He halted, thinking.

"Was that when you had these experiences?" Joe prompted him.

"That's right. They were very brief," Dad said, "even shorter than this time in Liverpool. I'd be in the

237

middle of doing something – I was eating dinner one time, I remember – and suddenly I'd be somewhere else. I didn't realise it was the past the first time, because there wasn't anyone nearby, and no houses. I was in the middle of fields, somewhere near our old house where you grew up. I could see the spire of the cathedral, and some sheep grazing, and then I was back at the table with my fork in my hand.

"The second time, I was out shopping when the street suddenly flicked into the past around me. It had to be several hundred years earlier, I guessed, from what people were wearing. It happened another three or four times after that, always in a different place."

"What did you think was causing it?"

Dad scratched his head. "At the time, I assumed it had been brought on by my sadness at Nain's death. Grief does funny things to people sometimes, though those episodes were a lot stranger than most people experience. I thought maybe as I began to come to terms with her being gone … I don't know, that doesn't make much sense, does it?"

"Did you stop wearing the St. Christopher?" Joe asked.

"Well, yes. I did. The catch broke, and I put it away. I only remembered about it when I was getting ready to move out. I bought it a new chain and gave it to you."

"Why me? Why not Sam?"

"I don't really know. I wasn't thinking very

clearly at the time, but maybe at the back of my mind I associated it with the past. You've always been much more interested in history than your brother."

Joe thought for a moment. "It was the St. Christopher all along, then," he said. "That first time, when you found yourself out in the fields near our house, you weren't *near* our house. You were on the spot where you'd just been sitting, in a time when our house and the houses around hadn't yet been built. That's how it works." He corrected himself, "How it worked."

"So did you say it had taken you to other worlds before this recent one?" Joe could hear the excitement growing in Dad's voice. "And you managed to stay in them?"

"Yes!" Joe felt a whoosh of delight at the thought of finally sharing it with someone!

"You lucky thing!" Dad cried. "Do you think I couldn't stay because I was already an adult by the time it happened to me?"

"Maybe. That sounds reasonable. You know those seizures I've been having for the last couple of years? That's what it was – I started passing out as I came back into the present."

"I wish you'd said!" Dad grinned. "All that fuss with hospital check-ups and everything! Your mum's been really worried. I must admit, I've been a bit concerned myself."

"I'm sorry," Joe said. "I knew I was fine, but

nobody was going to believe me, were they? Not even you! I mean, how could I tell you I'd been back to Roman Britain, or seen the Great Fire of London?"

"Romans? The Great Fire! Oh my goodness! And there was me teasing you about your historical fads when all that time you were researching the places you'd been! I want to hear all about it! Where else have you been? What was it like? What did you do there?" Dad's tongue was tripping over the questions.

Joe beamed. "I can't wait to tell you! I've been aching to talk to someone about it for over two years! Before I start though, shall I go down and fetch some mince pies? This is going to be a long night!"

"Good idea. I'll come down with you. There's a letter on the side you might be interested to see. It came this morning. Rather oddly, it was addressed to your mum, but at this address. I decided to open it."

Joe gaped.

"I must say, it's taken an age to arrive." Dad was laughing. "The postal service isn't what it once was! And what you'd written is rather baffling. I'd say you've got some explaining to do!"

18

Christmas Eve and Christmas Day were much better than Joe had expected. It was a huge relief to finally have someone else he could talk to about his time in the past, though it was frustrating having to wait until Sam was out of earshot. Dad was clearly avid to hear more, and so fascinated in the details that Joe found himself reliving his times with Lucy more thoroughly than he'd ever done before, as he tried to answer his father's unending questions.

It went a long way towards helping him come to terms with the knowledge that he would never travel back in time again. His grief at Lucy's death had eased too, both for being able to talk to Dad about her, and for having found her again here.

He still struggled to think of them as the same person. The polite, distant girl didn't seem anything like the one he'd come to love, except in appearance, but there was no point in grieving for someone who was still alive. One day, hopefully, he and Lucy would become friends. Joe told himself to bide his time. There was no rush.

While he helped Dad clear up from Christmas lunch, he was thinking about Mum instead. When he'd spoken to her on the phone this morning, she'd said she was spending the day with a friend. That probably meant she had a new partner, he realised. He wondered when she would be brave enough to tell him and Sam.

Imagine if it was someone else he knew from the past, he mused, as he emptied the dishwasher. There was no reason it should be, but now that Lucy had turned up here, Joe felt nothing would ever surprise him again. He considered the possible candidates: Harry Coles would be about the right age, or maybe George Penrose, though Joe hadn't actually set eyes on him this time. Morley, Tuffett and the air raid warden, Major Postlethwaite, were too old, while Jackson, Metcalfe, and Tobias were all thankfully way too young unless his mother's taste in men had dramatically changed.

All at once, an idea popped into his head. He laughed out loud.

"What's the joke?" Dad asked, looking round from the turkey stock he was making.

"It's not a joke. I just had a funny idea. I think Mum might have a new partner." Joe pulled a face. "Sorry! That wasn't the best way to break the news to you, was it?"

Fortunately, his father nodded. "Good. I was hoping that would happen," he said. "Have you met him?"

"No. I'm only guessing. She hasn't told us she's with someone yet. But I was thinking, imagine if it turned out to be Amos! That would be awesome!"

Dad frowned. "I'm not sure how I feel about being replaced by one of the most impressive men you've ever known! Couldn't you find someone weedy and pathetic from the past to step into Mum's life?"

Joe pretended to think. "Nope, sorry! Amos gets my vote!"

Dad's phone rang. He went out of the room. Joe could hear the rise and fall of his voice in the hall. "That was Ellen," he said, as he came back in. "She and the kids are going to come over in a bit for tea and cake, and maybe stay for supper. I said that was okay." He looked questioningly at Joe.

Sam had followed him into the kitchen. "That's great!" he said. "Peter and I can play my new game on the Xbox. He's got it already. He said it's really cool."

"Joe?" Dad cocked his head.

"Fine." Joe said, with forced brightness. He hadn't seen Lucy since the party and the thought of having to try again to win her round made his stomach flip flop. He would have liked to have a chance to prepare, rather than having it sprung on him, though exactly what those preparations might be, he didn't know.

"It'll probably be easier this time," Dad said. "In fact, it's very likely to be. Apparently, this was Lucy's suggestion. I think she wants to talk to you."

"Oooooh!" teased Sam. "You're in there, Joe! She must fancy you, though I can't think why!"

"Shut up!" Joe snapped.

"Thank you, Sam," Dad said. "We'll have none of that, please. It's not helpful."

"Hark at you both!" Joe's brother mocked. "It's not my fault if Joe's touchy! Seems to me, 'lurve' is in the air!" He pranced around the kitchen, making puppy eyes and panting.

Joe pressed his lips together. Anything he said would just sound like a feeble protest.

He turned back to Dad. "Did she say what about?"

Dad shook his head. "Ellen seems a bit mystified. I'm sure it's nothing to worry about." But his eyes betrayed the interest he'd kept out of his voice.

When they did arrive, two hours later, it wasn't obvious that Lucy wanted to be here at all. Peter and Sam disappeared at once to Sam's room, while Lucy sat upright on the armchair opposite Ellen. Joe watched her covertly while Dad and Ellen chatted. She seemed different this time, nervous rather than aloof. Why had she suggested they come?

After a few minutes, Ellen abruptly stood up. "Weren't you talking about refitting the kitchen?" she said to Joe's father. "Shall we have a look?" Dad and Joe both stood up too.

"It wouldn't interest you, Joe," Dad said, raising his eyebrows pointedly. "Why don't you entertain Lucy? I'm sure you can find something in common. An interest in history, maybe?" He winked at Joe as he left the room, closing the door behind him.

"Why did he say that?" Lucy asked, finally looking at Joe. Her cheeks were pink, as though she was embarrassed, though Joe was sure she hadn't seen Dad wink.

"I don't know." He sat down on the edge of the sofa cushion. "It's just something he and I like talking about, you know, what it used to be like to live at different times in the past."

Lucy's gaze grew more intense. "It's just that of all the things he might have said …" Her voice trailed off.

"Do you like history, then? Castles and ruins and things?" Joe was aware this wasn't the most obvious question to ask someone he'd only just met, but something about Lucy's face suggested it was the right place to start.

"Yes." She was still cautious.

"I like trying to imagine myself back into the past," he prompted.

"So do I!" A light came into her face. "Back to

when the place was swarming with people, all the clothes, the food, the different jobs everyone did, how they made things!"

"And the noises and smells!" Joe agreed with a grin. "Don't forget those! It was very different, wasn't it? I mean," he said hastily, "it *must* have been very different."

She gave him a piercing look. "It *was* very different," she said with emphasis. "Wasn't it?"

Joe stared at her. Was she trying to tell him what he thought she was telling him, that she remembered being there? Did she really remember those other lives she'd lived? But that wasn't possible, surely! She'd never remembered him when they met again, nor any of her earlier lives either!

Her next remark caught him totally off guard.

"We know each other already, don't we?" she said quietly. Her eyes strayed towards the door as though she was afraid of being overheard.

Joe's mouth fell open. He couldn't find the words to answer.

Confusion clouded Lucy's face. "Maybe we don't," she said hurriedly. "Maybe you just remind me of someone else I've met. Sorry, forget I said that. I made a mistake." She looked down at her lap, drawing up her shoulders as though hoping to disappear between them.

"No." Joe shook his head. "No, Lucy, you didn't. We do know each other. We're friends, aren't we?" His voice sounded stupidly hopeful.

Lucy looked up. She smiled. It was like the sun coming out. "Yes! We're friends. We've been friends for a long time, haven't we?"

Joe beamed at her.

"I just didn't expect you to remember," she went on. "You've never remembered me in the past. In fact, I wasn't expecting to meet you at all. Not here. Not ever again, actually, after you died."

"What? Me?" The smile slipped from Joe's face. "What do you mean? It's you who died!"

"Me?" Lucy echoed. "I'm not dead!"

"Nor am I!"

They looked at one another in bewilderment. The seconds stretched out.

At last, Joe said, "I think we need to start again, from the beginning. We do know each other. I've met you in the past, in Roman times first, then the Viking Age." He caught his breath. Had he really just said that? She was going to think he was mad! If his heart weren't thundering in his chest, he'd think he was having some sort of bizarre nightmare, where everything was about to go wrong!

"Not Vikings," she said firmly. "Anglo-Saxons!"

"Hey? No! You were definitely a Viking when I met you in Jorvik!"

"That's not right! I've never even heard of Jorvik! We were in Canterbury. You were a Saxon!"

Again, they stared at one another.

Joe tried to take in what she was saying. *He* had been a Saxon. *He* had been in Canterbury when she'd met him. As far as he knew, he'd never been to Canterbury. "When was that?" His words sounded frail and cracked. "When did we meet?"

"Three years ago, just after my dad died."

Joe thought back to three years ago. That was just before his parents had split up. He'd have remembered a trip to Canterbury, wouldn't he? But she'd said he'd *been* a Saxon. Not been dressed up as one. "When in history? What year, I mean?"

"604."

"But I've never been in that time!" he protested. "It was 82AD when I first met you. You were the daughter of Lucullus, living at Fishbourne Roman Palace."

Lucy blinked. "No! That can't be true! When was that in our world?"

"Two and a half years ago, the beginning of the summer holidays."

She flung herself back in the armchair and closed her eyes. Joe studied her face. This was his Lucy, behaving at last more like she usually would. Yet, their conversation had gone right off the rails of reality.

"You realise what's happened?" she said at length, opening her eyes. "We've both met before, quite a few times, in different parts of the past. But you don't remember the times where you lived there and I visited you, and I don't remember the times where I lived there and you visited me."

Joe frowned, trying to unravel what she was saying.

He nodded slowly. "I've met you seven times in all," he said, "starting as a Roman and then as a Viking. After that, we met at Old Wardour Castle in Henry the Eighth's time. You were rich then! The next time was the summer of the Great Fire of London. Then, in February this year we met in Bristol in 1792, and in the summer it was Victorian Cornwall.

"The last time was just last month," he went on, "during the bombing of Liverpool in 1940. That's when you were killed." He hesitated, then said sheepishly, "That's why I reacted the way I did when you arrived the other day. I was so happy to see you alive again!" He felt the colour rush to his cheeks.

Lucy's eyes brimmed with sympathy. "Oh, Joe! I'm so sorry. You must have thought I was really rude and horrible, when you only did what I'd have done in your shoes. The thing is, it was a massive shock for me! I had no idea it was going to be you – Mum hadn't told us anything much about you or Sam. I couldn't believe you were here, in my world, come back to life! I thought I was seeing things!"

Joe grinned awkwardly. "I thought you'd just decided I was weird. That would have been fair enough! But where have you met me? How many times?"

Lucy counted off on her fingers. "The first time was in Canterbury, like I said. After that it was London in 1483 – the year the princes disappeared from the Tower. Then we were in Plymouth just after the Armada had been sighted, and the time after that was during the Great Plague. That was awful!"

"We might have met!" Joe interrupted. "I mean, our modern day selves might have met. The Plague was still going on when I was there in 1666."

Lucy shook her head. "I was there before that – November 1665. You were living just outside the city walls. It was very grim. Red crosses painted on the doors and all that. One of your sisters died while I was there."

"But I haven't got any sisters!"

"Not now, you haven't," Lucy said. "The fifth time was Manchester in 1777. Did you know you had an earthquake big enough to ring the bells of churches around the city?"

"Really? No way!"

"Honest. Then it was Balmoral Castle up in the Highlands, when Queen Victoria was an old lady. Your father was a gamekeeper on the estate."

"Did you meet Queen Victoria?"

Lucy shook her head. "She wasn't there when I was, but you knew her quite well."

"Did I?" Joe gazed at Lucy. "I wish I remembered!"

"I wish I remembered the times you met me in the past, too," Lucy said.

"You said I'd died," Joe said. "How? Was that at Balmoral?"

"No. It was my seventh time back in the past, too. It might have been quite similar to your experience. It was April 1942, an air raid on Norwich. I've looked it up since. It was one of those raids they call the Baedeker raids." She paused. "It took me months to get over it, you being killed out of the blue like that. We'd become such good friends, even though you never remembered me when we met in each new time."

"You never remembered me either," Joe said. "And now neither of us remembers ourselves from the past!"

"At least we remember each other, though." She smiled shyly at him.

Butterflies rose in Joe's chest. He nodded.

"We might not share the same memories," she went on, "but this is better than not being able to talk about the past, isn't it?"

Joe nodded again. Such good friends, she'd said. And the way she'd said it, sort of longingly …

"You never know, maybe we could travel back in time together!" She grinned.

"I don't think I can," Joe said. "I gave away the thing that used to do it, at the end of my last time with you."

"That might not matter. I've still got mine." From inside the neck of her jumper, she pulled out a chain. A ring had been threaded onto it. "Here." She undid the catch of the necklace, and held the ring out.

Joe took it from her. "Where did you get this?" he asked, dumbfounded. He turned the smooth band over, running his thumb over the engraved pattern just as he'd done when he last held it.

Lucy laughed. "You gave it to me, in Canterbury, the first time we met."

"No, I gave it to you last time we met," he corrected her. "Well, nearly the last time – in the last world, anyway. I found it in the ruins in Liverpool, when we were exploring a bombsite."

"Really? That was quite a treasure to come by. It's Saxon. Didn't you realise? Mum and I took it to an expert to look at. I told them I'd found it on a beach, quite soon after you gave it to me."

Joe frowned. "But I only gave it to you last month, or in 1940, whichever you prefer."

"Well, I suppose 1940 came first! I don't think it makes any difference anyway. It's always been my key to the past, though I haven't used it since you died."

Joe held up the ring, marvelling at it. It gleamed in his palm, so much cleaner than when he'd seen it last.

"Well? Shall we?" Lucy was looking at him expectantly.

She came to sit beside him on the sofa and put her palm over his, pressing the ring between their hands.

"Are you ready? Where shall we go?"

THE END

THE FIRST BOOK IN *The Scar Gatherer* SERIES

THE
LEOPARD
IN THE
GOLDEN
CAGE

JULIA EDWARDS

THE SECOND BOOK IN *The Scar Gatherer* SERIES

SAVING
THE
UNICORN'S
HORN

JULIA EDWARDS

THE THIRD BOOK IN *The Scar Gatherer* SERIES

THE
FALCONER'S
QUARRY

JULIA EDWARDS

HAVE
YOU
READ
THEM
ALL?

THE FOURTH BOOK IN *The Scar Gatherer* SERIES

THE
DEMON
IN THE
EMBERS

JULIA EDWARDS

THE FIFTH BOOK IN *The Scar Gatherer* SERIES

SLAVES
FOR THE
ISABELLA

JULIA EDWARDS

THE SIXTH BOOK IN *The Scar Gatherer* SERIES

THE
SHIMMER
ON THE
GLASS

JULIA EDWARDS

THE SEVENTH BOOK IN *The Scar Gatherer* SERIES

THE
RING
FROM THE
RUINS

JULIA EDWARDS